Kickoff

KINGFISHER
a Houghton Mifflin Company imprint
222 Berkeley Street
Boston, Massachusetts 02116
www.houghtonmifflinbooks.com

First published in 2007
2 4 6 8 10 9 7 5 3 1

LIBRARY OF CONGRESS CATALOGING-IN-PUBLICATION DATA
has been applied for.

ISBN 978-0-7534-6082-5

Printed in India
1TR/1206/THOM/SCHOY/60BNWP/C

Kickoff

DONNA KING

Chapter 1

Hey, Lacey,

How are you doing, babe? How's Tampa Bay without me? How's the beach? And have you been down to the mall today? Did you check out the guys like we usually do—or like we usually did, *should I say?*

Tyra Fraser tapped away at the keyboard furiously. In her head she could picture sunshine and a blue sea. Outside her window she saw wet, gray clouds, gray slate roofs, and a muddy gray river.

Oh gosh, you don't know how much I miss Florida, she wrote. *England stinks. Specifically Yorkshire—specifically Fernbridge!*

How come you get to have a dad who runs a pizza place in the best shopping mall in the entire world and I have an army sergeant father who gets sent here? How dumb is that?

I mean, it's September, for God's sake, and it's freezing!!!!

Tomorrow I go to my new school. I am seriously gonna hate it, for sure.

Write me a long e-mail, Lacey. Give me your news, or I'll go crazy.

From your totally, 110 percent miserable friend,

Tyra!!!! xxxx

"Tyra, honey, could you come down?"

Tyra trailed downstairs to the tiny kitchen in the poky house they now called home.

"I need to iron your dad's shirts. Can you watch Shirelle?"

"I'll take her for a walk," Tyra said. Looking after her five-year-old, hyperactive kid sister in a space the size of a closet was asking for trouble. "C'mon, Shirry, let's go!"

No sooner did Tyra speak than the two girls were out on the main street, heading for the park. They walked hand in hand past the butcher's shop and the grocery store, down the hill, and over the old stone bridge. Shirelle pulled on Tyra's arm to stop her so that they could stand and stare at the flotilla of ducks swimming underneath the arch. She wanted to dash across the road to see them come out the other side, but Tyra held her back—luckily, because, just then, a guy on a motorcycle whizzed past.

This is one hick town! Tyra thought. *One main road. One bus stop. One play area with swings and a rickety jungle gym.* A few kids messed around in the park, kicking a ball and yelling.

"Push me!" Shirelle demanded, plonking herself on the closest swing. "I wanna fly! Push harder!"

"Hold tight," Tyra warned. She felt spots of cold rain on her face and looked up at the steep hill that rose almost sheer out of the narrow valley. A thick mist rolled toward them.

"Cool!" Shirelle squealed, her pink fluorescent sweater standing out against her light brown skin. Shirelle was the most colorful thing around, forming a bright downward arc in the dull air. She was into wild movement—running, leaping, splashing, yelling. She wasn't into sitting still, and boy, was she going to be a handful in her new school. Tyra was glad she wouldn't be there to see it. Instead, she'd be at the junior high school just down the road, along with a dozen other U.S. Army kids whose parents worked at the early-warning base out on the Yorkshire moors.

"Watch out!" a voice called.

She turned from the swings in time to see a ball flying toward her. It was going to be a direct hit on Shirelle, but at the last second Tyra jumped up and headed it to one side. The ball bounced away harmlessly.

A boy came running to get it. "Neat,"

he said with a surprised grin. "That was a cool header."

"Yeah, thanks."

Quickly, the kid picked up his ball and ran off.

For a while, Tyra watched them play. *Now, soccer!* she thought, once more remembering the Astroturf with the Florida sun beating down, Lacey in midfield neatly passing her the ball so that she could forge ahead past defenders and blast the ball past the goalkeeper and into the net. *Soccer is the one good thing about England! After all, it's the home of the greatest game in the world!*

"Higher!" Shirelle demanded, pushing with her feet and kicking her legs. "Tyra, make me fly!"

Hey, girl! Lacey e-mailed back later that evening. *This does not sound like the Tyra I know! What's with the misery, dude? Where's the go-getting, world-beating kid that I remember?*

Seriously, though, is it really that bad?

Okay, so the weather's not exactly wall-to-wall sunshine over there, but they have cool music, don't they? And you get to watch English soccer—Chelsea, Manchester United, Liverpool!

Yesterday I played striker for the Tampa Bay Butterflies—your old position. We won three–zero. I scored two of the goals. I know that sounds like we're not missing you, but we are—big-time! The girls said to say hi!

Okay, gotta go now, Tyra. Lots of luck tomorrow at the new school. Go, girl!

Love you—Lacey xxx

Walking into a place for the first time was always hard, Tyra told herself. The big glass entrance was buzzing with kids in uniforms, which was the weirdest thing. At her school in Florida, everyone had been able to wear whatever they wanted. Here, the boys wore dark green blazers and gray pants—*trousers*, Tyra thought, correcting herself. The girls wore white shirts and ties, with the same blazers as the boys. But they did the fashion thing with their skirts, wearing them short or long, narrow or wide, with their ties knotted loosely to show the top shirt button. Self-consciously, Tyra fiddled to loosen her own tie.

The corridor ahead was wide and crowded.

"Walk—don't run!" the teachers shouted. But the kids ignored them. They slung their bags inside their lockers, staring at Tyra and, by the scornful looks on their faces, giving her seriously low marks out of ten.

What's up? Do I have two heads? She glared back at a fair-haired girl who was giving her the evil eye.

"Are you the new girl?" the kid asked, looking like she was sucking on lemons. "It's time for attendance. Miss Jenkins said to get you."

Tyra nodded. Her long hair swung forward as she stooped to dump her bag inside a low locker. "Hey, I'm Tyra," she announced as she stood up straight. "I'm from Tampa, Florida."

The girl stared.

What did I say—that I came from Mars? Tyra wondered, already crushed.

It got worse as she was led into the classroom. There, 30 heads turned. Thirty faces stared. Thirty classmates seemingly wrote her off.

"There's an empty desk here at the front," the teacher told her without looking up. "Thank you for that, Alicia. Please be sure to show Tyra around for the rest of the day."

At the back of the room, Alicia leaned over from her desk and muttered darkly to her friends. At the front, Tyra swallowed hard and tried not to notice.

"Mikey Swales has got the hots for you, Alicia!"

"No way!"

"He does. He told me!"

"When?"

"At morning break. He asked me to tell you."

Tyra stood to one side of the group of girls who were giggling in the playground. She shivered in the cold wind. Already she'd been told to tie her hair back by the assistant principal and yelled at for not paying attention during math. The day was turning out even worse than she'd imagined.

"Anyway, Emma, you can tell Mikey that I'm not interested," Alicia scoffed. "I wouldn't be seen dead with a weedy little geek like him."

Tyra winced. *Poor Mikey!*

"He's not a geek," a girl named Molly protested. She was tall, like Alicia, and seemed more likely to stand up to her than Emma, who was Little Miss Mouse. "He plays on the boys' soccer team for a start."

"Well, Molly, *you* go out with him, then," Alicia shot back, making a beeline for one of the teachers on duty.

"It's not me who he's got the hots for!" Molly laughed, dragging Tyra along with the crowd.

"Hey, sir!" Alicia yelled.

The teacher took no notice, but walked on with his green fleece jacket zipped up to his chin, cradling a mug of coffee between both hands.

Alicia went after him. "Mr. Gray, we want to talk to you about the under-thirteen girls' soccer team!"

Soccer! Tyra's ears pricked up.

With a pained expression, the gym teacher turned. "Ah, yes, the under-thirteen girls. The magnificent eleven who were the under-twelves last year and didn't manage a single victory during all of last season!"

"That's because you concentrated too much on the boys!" Alicia reminded him. "You never gave us any real coaching."

Mr. Gray was obviously way past his sell-by date, Tyra decided. And he looked it, with his gray hair draped over his head to disguise his big bald patch, and his eye bags, and his belly hanging over his belt.

"Ah, the boys who won the English Schools Football Association Coca-Cola Cup!" he reminded Alicia. "That was the remarkably talented team I wasted so much time on last year!"

"Ha-ha, very funny, sir!" Alicia frowned. "Anyway, this year we want *real* coaching. Molly wants to go in goal, and Emma wants to be midfield defense. I'm a center forward—the main goal scorer!"

Yeah, why am I not surprised? Tyra thought. Alicia Webb had already gotten under her skin, and it was only day one. Back home in Florida, Tyra had been the top goal scorer of the Tampa Bay Butterflies.

Mr. Gray sipped his coffee and shook his head. "I don't have anyone in the department who's interested in coaching you girls, I'm afraid."

"But that's not fair," Molly pointed out.

"My mum says it's discrimination, and it's not allowed!"

Right on! Tyra thought.

"Whoa!" The teacher took a step back. "Quite the little feminist, aren't we, Molly Thomas?" His eye fell on a fellow member of staff who was patrolling the playground. He gave a cynical chuckle. "Then again, it doesn't have to be a member of the sports staff, does it? It could be, for instance, an *English* teacher!"

While Alicia shrugged at Molly and Emma, Mr. Gray beckoned to the passing teacher.

"Mr. Wheeler, just the man for the job!" he announced. "I know you're new to Fernbridge and you haven't gotten properly settled in yet, but I hear through the grapevine that you're the proud possessor of a Football Association coaching diploma!"

Blushing, the young teacher nodded. "Soccer's my thing," he acknowledged.

"He's young!" Alicia muttered.

"And cute!" Emma pointed out.

"Shut up and listen!" Molly told them.

Mr. Gray seized his chance. "Luck is on your side, girls! Mr. Wheeler here is a soccer coach. I'm sure he'd be willing to take on you girls!"

"Um—um—I would?" The chosen candidate seemed unsure.

"You would!" Mr. Gray insisted. "So, Mr. Wheeler, meet Alicia Webb, Molly Thomas, and Emma Dean, who will be the key players on your new team." He turned to Tyra with a vague look. "And you are . . . ?"

"Tyra Fraser," she stammered.

The shy new teacher smiled at the shy new student.

"Ignore her. She's from America. She doesn't play soccer," Alicia broke in as Mr. Gray walked off.

She does, actually! Tyra protested silently. *And she's good, if you only cared to ask!*

The English teacher looked down at Alicia. "Actually, I hear they play a lot of soccer at U.S. schools," he said.

Tyra nodded, but still couldn't speak. No, this was not a good start to her new school career.

"Oh, and good luck, Mr. Wheeler," Mr. Gray called from a distance. "Believe me, with these girls, you're going to need it!"

Chapter 2

Okay, Lacey, so this is the scene, Tyra typed. *It's a gym class, and we're out on the netball court or pitch or whatever it's called. I'm in a polo shirt and shorts, and it's 50 degrees out. A girl throws a ball at me—I catch it and run. The whistle blows, and everyone falls over laughing.*

What? What did I do?

"You mustn't run with the ball," the teacher tells me.

Huh? I mean, why not?

"This is netball, not basketball."

"Miss, her dad's at the army base. She's American!" Alicia Webb cuts in, like it's a big insult. She's laughing the loudest.

The teacher makes a cranky face and puts me on the sidelines. "Watch the game and learn the rules," she tells me, like I'm a total bonehead.

So I stand there in the wind, shivering and trying to figure out what's going on. It's day one, and I'm totally humiliated. I mean, totally.

Hey, Lacey, what happened to my life?

Write soon.

From your homesick friend, Tyra xxxx

P. S. Plus, they made me take off the friendship bracelet you gave me 'cause it's not part of the school uniform. Where do these people get off?!!

Tyra, you're the party girl par excellence! Lacey wrote back. *You love life. I'm thinking of you and remembering your smile—how you danced longer than anyone at Kari's pool party. Cool clothes, cool makeup, cool everything. Hot mama. Remember this the next time they stick you on the sidelines. And who's this Alicia girl? A big nobody, that's who.*

Hey, Tyra, you go into that school tomorrow and show them who you really are. I said it before and I'll say it again—you go, girl!

Missing you—Lacey xxx

★ ★ ★

"Shirelle, you have to put your shoes on!" Tyra insisted. It was the second day of school, and her sister was being a brat.

"No, no, no!" Shirelle yelled back.

"Yes. Mom's waiting in the car. You have to put your shoes on and go to school."

"I don't want to go!" Shirelle screamed every word, head back, face red with fury. "I hate it. I'm not going!"

Frowning, Tyra tried to sit Shirelle down and slip her shoes onto her feet. No way—the kid was kicking out and slithering off the chair and onto the kitchen floor.

Luckily, their mom came back in. "Okay," she said and sighed, "Tyra, you ask your dad to drive you. I'll work with Shirry on the idea of going to school today."

"No, no!" Shirelle yelled. She ran at her mom, fists flying.

That's what happened when your kid sister had attention deficit disorder and maybe autism—it threw the whole family into chaos. But Tyra was used to it, so she went to find her dad.

"You okay?" he checked as he drove her to school. His face never gave any sign of what he was thinking or feeling, and his army uniform took away even more of his personality.

"Yeah, I'm cool," Tyra replied.

"How was your first day?"

"Okay." Tyra knew not to complain. Her dad had no time for wimps.

"You found a friend yet?"

"Some," she lied.

"You joined any sports teams?"

"Dad, give me a couple of seconds, would you!"

He looked closely at her as she opened the car door. "Join a team," he advised. "Make some friends."

"So, Tyra, what does your dad do?"

Alicia came right up to her during homeroom, flanked on one side by Emma

Dean and, on the other, by a red-haired girl who Tyra didn't know.

"He's an army sergeant," she replied, realizing that Alicia must have seen the drop-off and that she was in for another bout of insults. What had she ever done to Alicia Webb?

"I get it—he's at the American army base, like that Tammy Chang kid who was here last year." Alicia folded her arms and tilted her head to one side. "The place on the moor with those spooky giant golf-ball thingies. Early warning or something."

Tyra nodded. Obviously, in the gospel according to Alicia, it was a major crime for your dad to work there. "He got posted here for two years."

"Wow, spooky!" Emma echoed, while the redhead pretended to shudder.

"So, who's coming to soccer practice after school tonight?" Alicia asked, suddenly brushing Tyra to one side as if she was a speck of dust. "It's Mr. Wheeler's first session."

"Me!" Emma said.

"Me!" said the redhead.

"Me, too!" Molly Thomas said from across the room.

"But I guess it's not your thing, Tyra." For a nanosecond, Alicia noticed the newcomer again. "Anyway, it seems like you'll have to focus on your netball this year!"

This brought a laugh from Emma.

"Actually, no," Tyra said, holding her voice steady. "I'll be coming along tonight."

"Whatever," Alicia muttered. Another quick flick cast Tyra way out of the conversation. "Hey, did you know that Mr. Wheeler's first name is Leo?" she told the others. "I looked him up on the school website under new members of staff. It says he was on the Leeds United junior team eight years ago."

"Then he's got talent!" Emma crowed. "So maybe he'll give us some real coaching for a change."

"Yeah, and this year our team is going

to go out there and win, win, win!" Alicia vowed. "With Leo coaching us—and me up front—we'll be unbeatable!"

Me, me, me! Tyra's thoughts turned sour every time she glimpsed Alicia. *Look at me! See how long my legs are. See how shiny my hair is when I swish it in front of my face!* "Yuck!" Tyra muttered out loud.

She was in the corridor, waiting to go into a room for their English class.

"Stand to the right!" a voice called from behind, and a tracksuited Mr. Gray pushed by, closely followed by Mr. Wheeler, who opened the door to their classroom. He waited while everyone filed in past him.

"Hello, sir!" Alicia flashed him a brilliant smile. "I'm glad you're our English teacher this year!"

Thrown off balance, the new teacher grinned awkwardly. Then he stopped Tyra as she made for an out-of-the-way desk at the back of the room. "Hello again, Tyra.

Are you settling in okay?" he asked.

She nodded and looked away.

"And you heard about soccer practice tonight?"

Another nod, but, with Alicia's eyes boring through her skull, Tyra didn't trust herself to reply.

"Good. So you'll be there?" Mr. Wheeler asked, making his way to the front.

"Yes, sir."

Sitting down next to Tyra, Molly gave a surprised sideways glance. "Is soccer really big in America?" she muttered.

"Huge," Tyra confirmed. "Before I came to England I played midfield/attack for the Tampa Bay Butterflies."

"Cool!" Molly grinned.

"So be there!" Mr. Wheeler told Tyra. "I'll see all of you who are interested in playing on the field at four o'clock sharp. Now, enough about soccer. Open your copy of *Romeo and Juliet*, and let's begin with the prologue."

★ ★ ★

Now Tyra didn't care that it was cold. She'd changed into her sweatpants and sweatshirt, and she'd laced up her soccer shoes.

She couldn't care less that Alicia had given her the cold shoulder in the changing room or that the boys' team had hung around outside making stupid, sexist comments as the girls ran out. Or even that Mr. Gray hadn't tried to stop them as he took his boys out onto the neighboring field.

"Go play in traffic, Adam Sutherland!" Molly had muttered at a boy wearing a goalkeeper's jersey. "Yeah, I know, that was *so* childish," she admitted to Tyra, who jogged beside her.

No, all that mattered to Tyra right now, in this moment, was that a ball lay at her feet and that Mr. Wheeler was giving his first instructions.

"I want you all to set off together and dribble your ball toward the goal. No fancy stuff—just good, solid dribbling to get yourselves warmed up. Basic skills—that's what we want to look at to start off with."

Tyra stood, poised. She smelled the wet grass trampled into the mud; she glanced up at the goal 50 yards away, listening for the whistle.

Focused on the ball, ready to run.

Mr. Wheeler blew his whistle. With Lacey's "Go, girl!" in her head, Tyra set off for the goal.

Chapter 3

The ball seemed glued to the toe of Tyra's shoe. She ran and dribbled, flicking the ball over the uneven ground, controlling it, and then sending it on across the turf. With her long legs, she surged ahead of the rest.

"Good job, Tyra!" Mr. Wheeler picked her out as the girls took shots at the goal.

Tyra's ball had found the back of the net, as swift and sure as a guided missile. Other kids took wild kicks and missed by a mile.

The coach joined them on the penalty spot. "Okay, shooting practice," he told them. "Put your ball on the spot and aim for the goal. Use your favored foot and blast it as hard as you can."

Alicia went first, naturally. She lined up

her ball and smashed it into the net. As she jogged to collect it, she flashed her best, brightest smile at the new coach.

Not bad, Tyra thought. *But I've seen better.*

Emma went next. She took a short run and booted the ball clumsily into the right side of the goal.

"Okay, Natalie, your turn." Mr. Wheeler nodded at Alicia's red-haired sidekick.

Natalie took her penalty and missed. Her face flamed up the same color as her hair.

"You took your eyes off the ball," the teacher noted. "Molly, you have a turn."

Faking the jitters, Molly took up position. "I'm going to miss!" she wailed. "Will Thomas's suspect temperament stand up to the pressure? The fans are willing her to score England's golden goal. Will she crack? Or will she score to become the nation's heroine?"

Tyra smiled to herself and watched Molly take a long run. Her shoe made contact, and the ball curved elegantly into the net.

"Phew!" She grinned, running to collect it.

The coach's smile showed that he'd enjoyed Molly's play-acting. "Okay, Tyra, let's see what you can do."

Better than most of these kids, she told herself, quietly placing the ball. She glanced up at the goal, judging the distance and the angle. *Whack!* She slammed her shot low into the left corner.

"Huh!" Alicia muttered under her breath. "Fluke!"

"Good job, Tyra. Good work, everyone." Mr. Wheeler handed out the praise. "Now, I want to see you working in pairs, one person dribbling the ball and the other tackling. Molly, you work with Emma. Natalie and Kim, Diana and Michelle, Alicia and Tyra . . ."

Tyra had dribbled; Alicia had tackled. Then Alicia had dribbled, and Tyra had gone in and taken the ball with ease. Turn and turn again. Every time Tyra had started with the ball, she'd dodged and turned, changed pace, and rolled the ball back under her foot to prevent Alicia from taking it away. But each time they switched and Alicia had tried to resist Tyra's challenge, Tyra had emerged triumphant.

"See that new kid? She's quick!" Adam said to Mikey Swales. The two boys stood on the sidelines, watching the girls.

"She doesn't look strong, though," Mikey pointed out. "A puff of wind would blow her over."

Adam disagreed. "It's not about strength if you're an attacker," he argued. "It's about agility and speed. And the girl's got loads of talent!"

Tyra had just robbed Alicia of the ball for the sixth consecutive time. She put her heart into every tackle, going cleanly for the ball.

This time, Alicia took a dive.

"Lady Alicia is not a happy bunny," Adam commented with a grin.

Alicia stayed facedown, spreadeagled on the muddy grass. Mr. Wheeler ran up to check that she wasn't hurt.

Alicia rolled over and held her leg, her face screwed up in agony. Tyra stood close by.

"Okay, take a break," the coach told Alicia, who hobbled off the field. "I like what I'm seeing," he told Tyra. "You're a natural athlete, a talented player. I reckon these other girls had better watch out!"

Breathing hard from the effort she'd put in, Tyra nodded her thanks. She caught sight of Adam and Mikey out of the corner of her eye. Adam gave her a big thumbs-up.

But Alicia limped up to the boys and began to complain in a voice that carried across the field. "Did you see that? Tyra chopped my legs out from underneath me—no intention of going for the ball! That would be a red card in anybody's book!"

"Yeah, she's a tough player," Mikey sympathized, obviously sucking up to Alicia. "Where did she hurt you?"

"On the ankle—whack! And all because I'd gotten past her . . ."

"Yeah!" Adam scoffed. "That wasn't the way I saw it. What I saw was a better player than you."

"And you're so-o-o the expert!" Alicia retorted over her shoulder, limping back onto the field as Mr. Wheeler gathered the group together.

"Okay, so I'm impressed," he told the girls. "I've spotted some real talent here, and I don't see any reason why we can't get a good team together for this season's Yorkshire League."

Breathless and excited, the girls beamed back at him. Emma sank onto the grass, hugging her knees to her chest. Molly zipped up her top and leaned shoulder to shoulder against Tyra. "Cool!" she gasped.

"When do you choose the team?" Alicia asked, getting down to the nitty-gritty.

The coach thought it through. "Let's see—this is Tuesday. We'll fit in another coaching session on Friday. Word will get around, and I expect more people will show up. By Monday, I should be in a position to start selecting."

There was a buzz of edgy excitement.

"God, I hope he chooses me!" Natalie murmured. "I was on the under-twelves last year, so I reckon I've got a good chance."

"My dad will kill me if I don't get on the team," Emma muttered.

As the group split up, Tyra noticed that only Alicia looked confident. She walked away with her head up, her sore ankle forgotten. "I'm going for striker," she reminded everyone. "That's my natural position."

"Oh, one more thing." Mr. Wheeler called them back. As he spoke, he seemed to look straight at Alicia. "The main thing to remember in this game is that you're playing as part of a team. You can have brilliant individuals with wonderful skills, but unless you're playing as a team, you're not going to win games."

Everyone nodded earnestly.

"Team spirit," the coach emphasized. "Passing the ball, thinking tactically, playing unselfishly."

"Yes, sir!" the girls chorused.

"Okay, you've got that." With a final nod of approval, Mr. Wheeler let them go. All except for Tyra. "Tell me more," he said, making her hang back and walk with him toward the school building.

"Huh?"

"Tell me where you played soccer in the States, who coached you, what position you played."

"I played for the Tampa Bay Butterflies. We were coached by David Lawrence."

"The ex-England and Manchester United star? That's bigtime stuff. The Butterflies—are they a junior team?"

"Yes, sir. Last year we won the Florida Junior Soccer Showcase in the under-thirteen age group. My best friend, Lacey

Imbergamo, and I were the youngest on the team."

"Impressive," Mr. Wheeler said. "But from what I've seen of the way you play, I'm not surprised. And how do you feel about playing soccer over here?"

Tyra took a moment to think about her answer and then let it all out. "If I'm completely honest, sir, I'm kind of struggling with the kids here, and the school rules, and the way the teachers speak, and the classes I have to attend. Plus, we have a few problems at home with my kid sister."

"Sorry to hear that," Mr. Wheeler said quietly.

"It's okay—I'm cool, sir. But since you asked me about soccer, my answer is that it's my life—always has been, always will be."

The young teacher nodded and smiled.

Tyra grinned back at him. "I've kicked a ball since the moment I could stand—I guess it came as naturally as breathing."

"Sounds like you've got a passion for it," Mr. Wheeler said, turning to head off toward the staff room. "It's good to hear that, Tyra."

"Thank you, Mr. Wheeler."

Here was her lifeline in this lonely new life. If she could do the thing she loved—play soccer and live in that moment—she knew she would survive.

As she watched the young teacher walk away, she called after him, "I mean it, Mr. Wheeler—thank you for asking me to play!"

Wednesday and Thursday had to be endured. At home Shirelle grew more furious about life, school—the whole darned thing.

"Today she kicked a boy in her class," Tyra's mom reported on Thursday evening. "The principal called me. He asked if we have any reports from the school psychologist back home."

Shirelle sat completely still, 12 inches from the TV screen. A cartoon played fast and furious.

"That's how she blocks out stuff," Tyra's mom said.

"For me, it's playing soccer." Tyra was hoping her mother would take the opening and talk to her, but she didn't. So she kept the argument that she'd had that day with Alicia to herself, when Alicia had accused her of sucking up to "Leo" and using dirty tricks to get selected for the team.

"You think it's so smart to go around with that 'poor me' look," she'd said in her loud voice, in front of a bunch of people. "I know you're doing it so Leo will feel sorry for you and pick you for the team, but, hey, it doesn't work like that!"

"I'm not . . . I don't mean to!" Tyra had protested. Then she'd beaten herself up for sounding so pathetic.

Alicia had flicked back her hair. "Oh, so that's how you normally look—like you hate everybody and think you're better than us!"

Ouch! Tyra had been lost for words.

"Back off, Alicia," Molly had cut in.

And Tyra had felt even worse for letting someone else fight her battles for her.

Now back at home, she left her mom brooding over Shirelle's school phobia and went upstairs to pick up a short e-mail.

Hey, Tyra, tell me some good news. Stuff is happening here. They're putting out hurricane warnings. Mom is uptight. She says if the electricity goes out like it did last year, she's through with living here. She wants to move to Colorado. My dad and I both say, "No way!"

Write back, babe. Lacey x

Hey, Lacey. The good news is that I'm playing soccer here in England. How cool is that? Our coach's name is Leo Wheeler. He's a teacher at school, and he's cool, too. On Monday he'll choose the team, and I hope I'm on it.

Tyra left out all the bad stuff about Alicia Webb. She didn't mention that a bunch of the kids trying out for the soccer team were untrained losers, or that no one had asked her over for a sleepover, or that they lived so far from a decent shopping mall that it meant a day trip, and her mom was too busy to take her.

So think of me spearheading the attack, picking up a ball from the left wing while avoiding the offside trap. Think of me scoring the winning goal!

Oh, and tell your mom to put up those shutters and ride out the hurricane. Thinking of you all. Tyra x

On Friday morning she got up, cleaned her soccer shoes, and headed into school with her dad.

Chapter 4

"Go, girl," Tyra's dad had said as she closed the car door. "You make striker on that soccer team, you hear?"

Huh, he remembered! Tyra was surprised. She'd told her dad about the new coach and the chances of her making the team in the middle of one of Shirelle's screaming fits. She didn't think he'd taken it in. But he had. She'd nodded at him and walked across the playground with her head up. *I'll be a striker on this team if it's the last thing I do!* she'd promised herself.

But she knew Alicia Webb still had other ideas.

"Listen to this! I'm guessing that Leo will choose you to play up front alongside me," Alicia told Natalie Heron during homeroom. "And to make my prediction come true, I'll throw in a couple of small tricks."

"Like what?" Natalie wanted to know. She, Emma, and Alicia were huddled by the radiator looking like the three witches from *Macbeth*. They whispered and cackled, casting eye-of-newt curses on their rivals in the buildup to tonight's second coaching session.

"Just watch me during English class!" Alicia boasted. "I'm going to be the most enthusiastic student ever. I bet you I can wind Leo around my little finger!"

Which meant that Tyra was forced to witness Alicia acting her socks off all through the balcony scene in *Romeo and Juliet*.

"O Romeo, Romeo! Wherefore art thou, Romeo?"

Alicia had bagged the female lead, shooting her hand straight up when Leo had asked for a volunteer, and now read the part with full-scale sighs and gasps. Tyra noted that some unsuspecting dude with zits, lurking at the back of the class, had been conscripted into reading the part of Romeo.

"With love's light wings did I o'erperch these walls," the boy mumbled.

"O'erperch—overperch—jump over," Mr. Wheeler explained as the boy stumbled and stopped. "It's a metaphor to show that love is such a powerful emotion that it can give Romeo wings to fly over the high wall and into Juliet's garden."

"How romantic!" Alicia sighed, getting into the spirit of the play.

"Cheesy!" Molly muttered, rolling her eyes at Tyra. "Yuck, Alicia!"

And after the class, Alicia was there in the playground, hanging out with the young teacher, faking a love affair with Shakespeare and putting him second only in her life to soccer. "Sir, have you chosen the girls' team yet?" she simpered.

"Not until Monday," Leo reminded her.

"Yeah, but you must already have an idea of who's going to head up the attack with me."

Mr. Wheeler gazed serenely into the distance and said nothing.

"I took on board what you said about team spirit and thought I'd better let you know how well Natalie and I played together last season. We kind of have this paranormal ability to read each other's moves on the field."

So how come you and Natalie never scored any goals? Tyra wondered. She was frowning, but started to grin at Molly when she stuck her fingers down her throat and pretended to be sick.

"I'll bear that in mind, Alicia," Mr. Wheeler told her, striding away quickly.

Then there was lunch break, and Alicia and Natalie were out on the glistening wet playground, looking so enthusiastic and unexpectedly glamorous in their green, white, and black school tracksuits. They sprinted and jogged, dribbled and tackled, all in full view of the staff-room window, to make sure that Mr. Wheeler could see how committed they were.

"Wow, look at the legs on Alicia!" Mikey drooled.

In the afternoon there was more boring school, and then finally—and to Tyra's relief—the bell rang to end the day.

She went straight to the changing room, laced her shoes with eager fingers, and trotted out into the wind and rain.

"Scram, girls! I booked the Astroturf for the boys' training session!" Mr. Gray barked and chased the girls off the Astroturf, onto the muddy grass field beside it.

"When did you do that?" Mr. Wheeler challenged. He wore a silver whistle hanging from a red ribbon and an all-black Adidas tracksuit.

"Yesterday." Mr. Gray lied and turned his back. "I signed up for it on the staff-room notice board."

Mr. Wheeler shrugged and gave in. "It looks like we're going to have to do our best in the mud," he told the girls. "Today I want us to focus on passing the ball. Let's make our passes long and accurate, working in the same pairs as last time."

Inwardly, Tyra groaned. No doubt this would mean more of Alicia's faked falls and prima-donna displays. Why did the coach keep on pairing up the two of them? Couldn't he see that they hated each other's guts?

For this first routine Tyra dribbled the ball from the goal up to the 25-yard line and then passed it to Alicia on the center line. The ball landed neatly at Alicia's feet and stuck in the mud, making Alicia fumble it. "What was that?" she yelled back at Tyra. "Call that a pass?"

Emma and Natalie snickered.

When it came to Alicia's turn to pass ahead to Tyra, she flicked the ball way too short and then laughed as Tyra ran back to collect it. "You didn't read that one very well, did you, Miss Tampa Bay Butterfly!"

On the sidelines Mr. Wheeler stood and made notes in a small spiral-bound pad.

So far, Tyra had held her tongue. Okay, she'd love to yell back and give it to Alicia straight—*Back off, you egomaniac! Stop throwing your weight around and focus on passing the ball accurately, for Pete's sake!* But all her life she'd been taught self-control.

"Never let your feelings overrule your head on the sports field," her dad had told her. "Feelings get in the way of winning, and whether it's swimming in a race, dunking the ball in the basket, or driving the soccer ball between the goalposts, winning is the only thing that matters. That's what you're out there to do!"

Tyra had learned her lesson well. *Don't argue with the referee. Don't badmouth your opponent (never mind your teammate!).*

"Okay, so now we're going to work on the defender tackling the striker from behind,"

Mr. Wheeler announced. "Remember, always go for the ball, never the player. A good, clean tackle is what we're looking for here."

The group of girls took up their starting positions in the goalmouth. Their shoes were caked with mud, and their shorts and shirts were covered in the stuff. Still, they set off in pairs, with Tyra and Alicia the third in line.

"Okay, Tyra, go!" Mr. Wheeler ordered when their turn came.

Tyra ran confidently with the ball, covering the ground as fast as usual.

"Okay, Alicia!" Mr. Wheeler said.

Alicia sprinted after Tyra, trying hard to make up the gap.

Tyra heard her coming, but she never took her eyes off the ball. She flew on, dribbling the slippery ball with ease.

"Lousy showoff!" Alicia muttered from behind. "You're supposed to let me tackle you!"

Sure! Tyra thought. *You catch me first, and then you can tackle!*

Coming up from behind, Alicia was breathing hard. In desperation, she lunged into a sliding sideways tackle. Alicia's shoes crunched into Tyra's left ankle. Tyra fell awkwardly, with Alicia on top of her. The ball skidded over the sideline and came to a stop at the young coach's feet.

"The ball, not the player!" Mr. Wheeler reminded Alicia sternly. He waited for the two girls to pick themselves up out of the mud.

Tyra winced as she stood up and tried to put her weight on her left foot. Her head spun, and she felt sick in the pit of her stomach. *Ow, that hurts!* She stooped to roll down her thick sock.

"Wimp!" Alicia muttered as Mr. Wheeler ran up with a can of anti-inflammatory spray.

Ignoring Alicia, Tyra sat back on the ground, eyes closed, trying not to give in to the pain. She nodded when Mr. Wheeler asked if she was okay. He sprayed the spot, tested the movement in the ankle joint, and asked her to stand up, which she did. "Can you keep playing, or would you rather sit out?"

"Keep playing," she told him. Gingerly, she put her right foot on the ground and jogged away, favoring her left foot.

"Okay, Alicia, I want you to take some time out during the next exercise," Mr. Wheeler instructed. "Think about what you did wrong. Tyra, you team up with Molly in goal and put in some shooting practice. But, before that, I want to remind everyone about the English Schools Football Association game list that I asked Emma to pin up on the sports notice board yesterday morning. Did you all get a chance to look at the ESFA letter?"

"Yes, sir!" the girls sang out—all except Tyra.

How come no one told me about that? she wondered. Then she noticed Alicia's sly glance at Emma and realized why she'd been kept out of the loop. "No, sir, I didn't," she announced. "Where exactly is the board?"

"Didn't Emma show you like I asked her to? It's in the corridor outside the girls' locker room." Mr. Wheeler took a piece of paper from his pocket and read from it. "So, anyway, the first game is against Darnley Junior High. It takes place here at Fernbridge a week from today. That's Friday the thirteenth . . ."

There were gasps and superstitious groans. "Friday the thirteenth! . . . Oooh, scary!"

"We don't believe in any of that bad-luck stuff!" Mr. Wheeler told them briskly. "We're going to field a team equal to anything Darnley can throw at us, and I'll be ready to announce it first thing on Monday morning. So check that notice board again, all of you!"

"Yes, sir!" came the chorus of eager voices. A total of 20 girls were battling for 11 places on the team. Despite the mud, the wind, and the rain, not a single one wanted to be left out.

"Good. Now back to work," Mr. Wheeler told them. "Molly, get in goal. Tyra, see if you can beat the goalie and slam that ball into the back of the net."

Chapter 5

Choose me! Choose me! Choose me! Tyra practiced her silent mantra as she and Shirelle walked through Darnley Shopping Center the following day. *I'm good. I'm really good!*

Her mom had driven the girls into town and dropped them off outside the mall. "Don't let Shirry out of your sight," she'd told Tyra in a stressed voice.

Tyra had promised to hold Shirelle's hand, but the kid soon slithered free. Already she'd disappeared inside a shoe store, a hair salon, and a clothes store, and each time she had to be dragged out screaming and yelling—three vanishings in the space of 15 minutes; almost a world record, even for Shirelle. "Come on," Tyra told her now, dragging her into a Claire's Accessories. "Let's go look at some bling!"

I'm good, Mr. Wheeler! Choose me! Tyra inspected the necklaces and bracelets while Shirelle wrapped a wide, shiny black belt around her waist, covering it in fingerprints.

"Are you going to buy that?" a suspicious sales assistant asked.

"No. Give back the belt, Shirry. C'mon, give it back!"

"No, no, no!" The kid set up a crazy tug of war over the belt. People stared.

Oh, no, just my luck! Tyra caught a glimpse of the very person she didn't want to see—Alicia Webb had just stepped out from behind a rack of scarves. "Let go, Shirry!" she muttered.

"No. I want it!" *Tug, tug, tug!*

"You can't have it. We don't have any money to buy it."

Tug. "Give it to me!" Shirelle screamed.

Of all the people in the world who could be watching this, it had to be Alicia and a couple of her blingy friends! Tyra sighed, let go of her end of the belt, and watched her crazy sister fall back onto the floor with a thump. The assistant jumped at the chance to move in and grab the belt.

Meanwhile, Alicia and her pals swanned across the floor toward Tyra. Alicia raised her perfectly plucked eyebrows and smirked.

"Poor you!" she commiserated, glancing at Shirelle, who was moving up a gear into full tantrum mode.

"Shirry, stand up. Quit that!" Tyra ignored her rival and struggled with her wailing sister. "I'm sorry!" she told the assistant. "Sometimes she can—y' know—well, she's . . ."

". . . Totally nuts?" Alicia offered to finish Tyra's sentence.

The two friends laughed loudly. Then the three girls walked on, giggling and looking back over their shoulders.

Tyra closed her eyes and sighed. She hauled Shirelle to her feet.

"It's okay—don't take any notice of them." The assistant changed her tune. She now obviously felt sorry for what Tyra had to put up with.

"Shirelle has ADD," Tyra explained quietly. "And they think maybe she's autistic."

The woman nodded. "I saw a TV show about that. It's hard."

"It's cool, thanks." Squatting down to Shirelle's level, Tyra wiped the tears from her sister's face. "Are you okay now?"

Shirry nodded. Her little face looked completely sad and confused.

Tyra smiled, trying to bring her back into the world. "Come on, sweetie pie, let's go find a McDonald's," she said.

Hey, Tyra,

Hurricane Alicia has hit Tampa Bay. She tore up houses on the waterfront along Sand Dollar Drive. Your old house lost its roof. Ours didn't take a direct hit, thank God. Downtown is a mess—the mall's flooded; my dad's place has no electricity, no fresh water, no gas.

Tyra read the start of Lacey's e-mail three times over.

Hurricane Alicia—how random was that!

Dad's out in the yard right now, trying to save the wrecked awning. Mom's stocking up on bottled water before the stores run out. Our game against the Miami Gazelles is canceled. We beat them two–zero last year, remember?

Hey, how are you doing over there in Merry Olde England? Did you try out for the soccer team yet? You show them, girl!

Tyra typed a long reply before she left for school on Monday morning.

Hi there, Lacey!

So Alicia did her worst, and you came through. I saw the TV reports. It stinks that our old house got hit. I feel bad about that.

Guess what? I have my own private

hurricane over here, and she's also named Alicia. This one is human, but is a force of nature too. She comes at you like a whirlwind and batters anything that stands in her way—specifically me! I don't get why she doesn't like me—except that:

a) I'm aiming to take her position on the school soccer team
b) I'm new to the school and I'm American
c) I have a crazy kid sister
d) My dad's in the U.S. Army . . .

Enough already!!!

Hey, I don't care—I'm gonna make that team.

Today is the Big Day—names are posted on the board. I'm so totally freaked out! Wish me luck.

Always your best-ever friend, Tyra xxxx

Eight-thirty A.M. The area around the notice board was crowded with girls. Everyone strained to read the names on the team.

"Molly, you're in goal!" Alicia cried.

She stood at the front and blocked everyone's view.

"Cool!" Molly stood at the back and punched the air.

Tyra stood to one side, eyes closed, silently chanting her mantra. *I'm good. Choose me!*

"Emma, Kim, Helen, and Michelle are defenders!" Alicia announced.

"Congratulations, Emma!" someone behind Tyra said. "I knew you'd make it!"

"Hurry up, Alicia, read out the rest!" Natalie pleaded.

"Sorry, Nats—he's chosen you to play in midfield." Alicia's forefinger ran down the list. "Diana, K. D., and Sara—you're there too! And Laura and Rebecca are down as subs."

"Wow, cool! . . . Yeah! . . . I'm in! . . . So cool!"

"That makes nine regular players on the team," Molly muttered, crossing her fingers for Tyra. "Come on, Alicia, who are the final two?"

"Me, of course!" Alicia said, turning to face the huddle of eager faces.

"And?" Molly prompted.

Alicia's eyebrows knitted together in a slight frown. She gave a shrug.

"Oh, move out of the way!" Pushing to the front, Molly read the list. "It's you, Tyra!" she called out. "Here it is in black and white—Tyra Fraser. You and Alicia are going to spearhead our attack!"

Yes! Tyra's spirits lifted; her heart sang all around school that whole day. *He chose me! I'm on the team!* She bathed people in smiles, she joked, and she joined in with her classes like she'd done back home.

"Something tells me you're settling in better this week," Mr. Wheeler said to her during Act II, Scene 3 of *Romeo and Juliet.*

"Yeah!" She grinned. *What is it with these people?* she wondered. *I achieve my heart's desire, I'm floating on air, on cloud nine, totally blissed out, and they call it "settling in"!*

She floated through the school day and

then went home and told her mom. "I made the soccer team."

"Good job!" her mom said, as if there had never been any doubt.

"We play our first game on Friday. Some of the players are completely untrained. You wouldn't believe how much work we have to put in before then."

"I guess you're right." Tyra's mom had just come off the phone. She wasn't paying too much attention to Tyra's news. Shirelle was glued to cartoons as usual.

Tyra continued. "I need to get in shape for a start." And the whole team definitely needed as much coaching as Mr. Wheeler could fit in. They should also talk tactics and take a look at the strengths and weaknesses of the Darnley Junior High team, Tyra thought excitedly.

"Sure, honey . . . That was another call from Shirelle's principal." Serena Fraser sighed and shook her head. "Your dad and I need to have a serious talk."

Tyra frowned. "I'm going out for a run," she said.

"Sprint!" Mr. Wheeler stood in the gym and yelled instructions. "Okay, now jog! . . . Sprint! . . . Jog!"

"I'm *so* not in shape!" Molly groaned as she ran alongside Tyra. "Hey, how come you haven't even broken a sweat?"

"I guess I'm used to this," Tyra replied calmly. "Our coach back home believed in peak fitness."

"Pushups, on your knees!" the coach instructed. "Okay, ready—one, two, three, four . . ."

"Ouch!" Natalie collapsed on the floor after 12 pushups.

"Thirteen, fourteen, fifteen . . ."

The other girls groaned and gave in. Tyra, Alicia, and Molly kept going.

"Twenty-one, twenty-two, twenty-three . . . Good work, Tyra . . . twenty-four, twenty-five . . ."

Tyra alone made it past 30.

"Lousy showoff!" Alicia muttered under her breath.

It was Tuesday, and the weather was too bad for them to train outside. Inside the gym, the Fernbridge girls' team members pushed their bodies to the limit.

"Okay, gather around." Mr. Wheeler gave the girls a break so that he could start talking tactics. "The important thing is for us to take the game to the opposition," he began. "We don't want to play defensively—we have to attack!"

"Yes, sir!" Alicia chipped in. "I need a good supply of passes from the midfielders!"

Mr. Wheeler nodded. "Kim and Natalie, I want you to work down the left-hand side of the field, feeding passes to Alicia. Sara and K. D., you have to supply Tyra on the right."

Tyra listened hard. She thought that with a little extra coaching, K. D. would be good, that they would work well together. In her head, she could visualize some neat teamwork between them.

"Defenders, I want you to mark the opposition closely—never let them find the spaces. Play tight, tackle solidly." Mr. Wheeler went through the team, giving each player strict instructions. When he came to Molly, he asked her a question. "How confident do you feel about being in goal?"

"I'm cool," she replied.

"Good. Your reactions are pretty fast back there. And you catch the ball well—you have a safe pair of hands. But work on your goal kicks, okay?"

"Yes, sir!" Molly was up and ready to put Mr. Wheeler's advice into practice.

"Not now," he said with a grin, glancing at his watch. "Look at the time. You all have homes to go to, don't you?"

Reluctantly, the girls shuffled out of the gym.

"I ache all over!" Emma groaned as they hit the changing room.

"Me, too!" Natalie slumped on a bench.

"Yeah, Leo's seriously into fitness." Reaching for her towel, Alicia gave Tyra a cold stare. "All those stupid pushups—it's a bit over-the-top if you ask me."

Tyra couldn't help herself. "No," she argued. "We need to build up our fitness. It's the bottom line."

"Oh, the bah-dum line!" Alicia sneered, copying Tyra's accent. "Funny, I thought the bottom line was scoring goals and winning games!"

The noise in the changing room died away as Tyra and Alicia went head to head.

"Uh-oh!" Molly muttered, grabbing her towel and escaping into a shower stall.

Emma and Natalie lined up behind Alicia.

"What is it with you, Alicia?" Tyra demanded. "What's with the nasty looks and putdowns?" *Wrong!* she thought. *I'm getting myself into a fight with Alicia here, and we're supposed to be on the same team!*

"Well, if you don't know, I'm not going to

tell you!" Alicia retorted. Then she changed her mind, launching into an attack. "You know what your problem is, Tyra? You're so into yourself, you can't even see it. I mean, bigheaded doesn't even get close to the way you act. It's worse—it's total arrogance, like you're the only person who's ever played in a soccer game! Like you're the superstar!"

"Yeah," Emma echoed. "It's always the Tampa Bay Butterflies this, the Tampa Bay Butterflies that! And you've only been here five minutes."

Shocked, Tyra backed off, edging toward the door. "Is that the way it looks?" She appealed to K. D., who shrugged and turned away.

"Not *looks*. It's the way it *is*!" Alicia insisted.

"But . . ." Tyra shook her head. Then she realized that what she'd privately been thinking about the novice players must have shown in the way she'd been acting. All that "I'm-good-choose-me stuff" had really gotten on her teammates' nerves.

She needed to hold back on that in the future, she realized.

"Cat got your tongue? That's a first!" Alicia sneered. "You usually say plenty."

Okay, enough! Despite her good intentions, Tyra walked back toward Alicia, staring her down. "Hey, girl, it's yourself you're talking about. *You're* the only prima donna around here! Talk about arrogant!"

There was a general gasp. All eyes were fixed on Alicia and Tyra.

"Seems to me you need a reality check," Tyra went on. "So, okay, Alicia, you led the team last year and you got used to telling everyone what to do. But you didn't actually win anything, did you?"

"Ouch!" Molly said from inside the stall.

It was too late for Tyra to back off, so she went on. "Not a single game, from what I hear. And to me, the reason's simple—you didn't have good coaching and you didn't know how to work as a team."

"What did I tell you?" Alicia appealed to

Emma and Natalie. "Didn't I say she was totally into herself?"

But for once her two allies wouldn't look her in the eye.

"Well, this year we do have a coach—and he's good," Tyra pointed out. "So we have to work with him and get serious about winning."

"Yeah!" a couple of girls murmured. Everyone looked at Tyra with new respect.

"Starting with Darnley Junior High," Tyra reminded them. She took deep breaths, feeling good about speaking her mind. For the first time since she'd arrived at Fernbridge, her focus was back in the right place. "Let's go out there on Friday and score some goals!" she said.

Chapter 6

"So, are you coming to watch us on Friday?" Molly asked Mikey and Adam.

The two boys had been looking on as the girls trained on Wednesday after school. After the training session, they'd tagged along with Molly, Tyra, and a few others.

"Mikey will definitely be there!" Adam joked. "It's like 'Mary Had a Little Lamb'—'Everywhere that Alicia went, Mikey was sure to go!'"

Mikey blushed and then elbowed Adam in the ribs.

"So, Adam, are you coming to watch the game or the girls?" Molly demanded.

"The game, what do you think?" He laughed, veering off down the road and tugging Mikey after him.

"How come they don't take us seriously?" Tyra wanted to know. She was still on a high after her selection for the team and her face-off with Alicia. And a tough coaching session had raised her hopes of putting on a good show on Friday.

"Because they're boys!" Molly answered, as if that explained everything.

Tyra laughed. "Yeah, I guess!"

"I saw Mr. Gray teasing Mr. Wheeler about us earlier," Molly went on. "He was laughing at how seriously Mr. Wheeler was taking things, saying that he'd have to wave a magic wand if he wanted us to win any games this year."

Tyra frowned. "I guess we'll just have to prove him wrong. So you think Mr. Gray really doesn't want us to succeed?"

"Yeah. Imagine him having to admit that the girls are better than the boys!"

"Jealousy!" Tyra sighed.

Molly nodded. "Right. But what the

old rottweiler doesn't realize is that if you're jealous, you put yourself in a lose-lose situation."

"Meaning?"

"No one wins. Take Alicia." Pulling Tyra to one side and walking into the park as the others went on down the street, Molly spoke in a whisper. "You realize Alicia is crazy jealous over you, don't you? That's what's behind the nasty comments."

"I guess."

"Well, she can't win this one, see? If you score loads of goals for our team, she loses face. But if you don't and our team keeps on losing games like we did last year, she still loses—get it?"

"So if she can't win, why do it?" Tyra was way out of her depth as far as Alicia Webb was concerned.

Molly paused, pursed her lips, and delivered her verdict. "Because she can't help herself. She's out of control."

Tyra gazed across the park at the empty

swings and the colorful leaves on the trees across the river. For the first time she realized how pretty the place was—like New England in the fall. She was grateful to Molly for going out on a limb and confiding in her like this, but it didn't make easy listening. "That doesn't sound good," she said and sighed.

"It isn't," Molly confirmed. "If I were you, Tyra, I'd watch out for Alicia's next move. And be ready for it when it comes!"

Okay, so Tyra realized there were problems, both at home and at school.

By Friday her parents had completely given up on getting Shirelle into school. They'd made an appointment to meet with the principal on Monday.

"It's too much!" Serena had cried on the Thursday night. Real tears, real angst over what to do about Shirry, who was, as usual, blocking the world out with wall-to-wall Disney.

Tyra's dad had been a shoulder to cry on, but he hadn't come up with any solutions. That morning, he'd dropped off Tyra at the school gates.

"Wish me luck," she'd reminded him as she lifted her sports bag from the back seat.

He was out of uniform, dressed in a gray sweatshirt and black jogging pants. "Huh?" he'd muttered.

"For the soccer game tonight. Wish me luck!"

"Go, girl!" he'd told her, without meaning it.

Then Tyra had walked straight into her major school issue—namely Alicia in hyper mode.

"Obviously, I'm the team captain!" she announced during homeroom.

"Who says?" Molly wanted to know. "Mr. Wheeler didn't mention it!"

"I was the captain last year, so it goes without saying that it's me again!" Alicia glared at Tyra, who hadn't said a word.

"Okay, so we'll ask him before the game tonight," Molly decided.

"And don't get any ideas about sneaking off to see Leo behind my back, Tyra Fraser!" Alicia warned out of the blue.

Tyra shrugged. "I don't even want to be the captain!" But she realized it was a lie even as she said it.

Alicia's eyes bored into her. ". . . Just don't!"

Then Miss Jenkins began to take attendance, and everyone fell silent.

It was like that all day—Alicia picking on Tyra, who tried not to retaliate, Alicia freezing Tyra out of conversations, Alicia snickering at Tyra behind her back. By the time school ended, Tyra was stressed out. She got changed for the game into black shorts and a green shirt with a neat black design on the back and a logo on the front showing the Fernbridge crest. The long socks were patterned with black-and-white hoops. The uniforms smelled new as Tyra and the rest of the team put them on.

"I raided the PTA fund to buy new uniforms because I thought you deserved it," Mr. Wheeler told them as they trotted out onto the field. "You look like winners, girls—you're looking good!"

But not feeling it, Tyra thought. She was angry with herself for letting Alicia get to her. And she still had zero confidence in some of the players on the team.

Mr. Wheeler gathered them around for a talk session. "The Darnley bus has just arrived," he told them. "Their team is getting changed as I speak."

A shiver of anticipation ran through the group.

"I have one last thing to do before we kick off," the coach went on. "And that's to hand out the captain's armband."

Tyra held her breath along with everyone else. Out of the corner of her eye she could see Alicia preparing to step up.

"The captain's job is to keep the team together out there on the field," Mr. Wheeler reminded them. "I've thought long and hard about this responsibility and have come to the conclusion that, because of her experience and skills, Tyra is that person."

Tyra felt her jaw drop. Alicia's shoulders sagged, and her head fell forward. Everyone else whispered and nudged.

"Come and get it," Mr. Wheeler said, offering Tyra the band.

Silently, she slipped it on. There was no time to think, because the Darnley team was coming onto the field. They were in white uniforms with blue trim—mostly tall girls, who seemed to be brimming with confidence. Their coach was a middle-aged woman dressed in jeans and a red fleece jacket.

"Okay, join hands in a circle," Mr. Wheeler told the Fernbridge girls. "Heads down, lean in toward the middle."

As luck had it, Tyra linked up with Alicia, whose hands were trembling and whose face was deadly pale. For some reason, this show of nerves caught her off-guard. "Hey, take it easy," she murmured. "It'll be fine."

"Don't even speak to me!" Alicia muttered back.

Then Mr. Wheeler reminded them why they were there. "What do we want?" he asked.

"We want to win!" the team chanted.

"When do we want it?"

"Now!"

They broke up with a round of high-fives and ran to take up their positions. The referee blew the whistle, and the game began.

First-half jitters made a mess of both teams' play.

Darnley passed the ball better, but their attack lacked focus. Fernbridge tackled well, but there was no formation behind their play, and their set moves from corners fell apart.

Five or six times Tyra outran her opponents, swerved, and dummied to arrive in the goalmouth, only to find herself faced with four Darnley defenders and no Fernbridge players in the box with her. So where was Alicia when she needed her?

And then there was the problem with midfield. Whenever Sara or Natalie or Kim got the ball, they passed to Alicia, who wasn't always in a good attacking position. Only K. D. tried to feed the ball to Tyra.

Okay, so they're freezing me out of the game, Tyra decided. And she was pretty sure she knew why. This was what Alicia had told them to do, and what Alicia said, Natalie, Sara, and Kim did!

Meanwhile, the Darnley players were finding their rhythm. Just before halftime they got in a couple of shots, and Molly had to pull off two good saves.

"Good job!" Tyra ran up to pat her on the back after the second attempt. It was still zero–zero, but Fernbridge was lucky that they weren't at least one goal down. The whistle blew for halftime.

As Tyra ran up the field for the team talk, she picked out a few familiar faces in the sparse crowd. Mikey and Adam were there as promised, along with a few of their buddies from the boys' team. Behind them, Mr. Gray was standing with another teacher. He had his hands in his pockets, a gray woolen hat pulled down over his eyes, a checked scarf around his neck, and a sneer on his face. A few parents had also come to watch their girls play.

"What happened?" Mr. Wheeler demanded, palms spread, a look of disbelief on his face. "Did you forget everything we worked on during the week?"

The team hung their heads. Tyra took out a bottle of water and drank deeply.

"You're completely out of shape," the coach chided. "Natalie and Kim, you have to mark your opponents more closely. And stop booting the ball wildly in the hope of finding Alicia up front. Most of the time she's in an offside position anyway."

"No way!" Alicia muttered. She glowered at Tyra.

Mr. Wheeler turned to his captain. "Tyra, you need to show leadership. Organize your players for the set pieces. Don't be afraid to dish out the orders."

She nodded and took another sip. Okay, so Sara, Natalie, and Kim had forgotten all their tactics, but they were eager to win, and she could spot real talent in Kim especially. She took Kim to one side and urged her to pass forward on both wings.

"It's not that you're playing badly as individuals." The coach concluded his halftime tips. "Alicia, I've seen some nice moves from you, and Molly, you put in a couple of excellent saves."

Molly grinned and accepted high-fives from Sara and Michelle.

"But you're not coming together as a

team," Mr. Wheeler warned.

Tyra nodded. She knew he was right on target. "Okay, let's go!" she urged, running back onto the field ahead of the rest. "Let's do it. Let's win this game!"

Darnley's coach had done a good job on her team during their halftime talk. They came out with their heads high, ready to run after every ball, going hard into each tackle.

But Tyra knew that Fernbridge, despite their rough edges, could beat them. "Good job, K. D.! Nice tackle!" She yelled encouragement to her team, signaled positions for them to take up, ignored Alicia's hostile stares. "Emma, stay back. Kim, move forward. Alicia, you're offside!"

"Good!" Mr. Wheeler called to her from the sidelines.

"Go, Fernbridge!" Mikey, Adam, and the boys cheered.

Still the score stayed at zero–zero.

The Darnley forwards pressed hard. Tyra

sent Sara and Diana deeper into defense. On a Fernbridge free kick, she signaled for K. D. to ignore Alicia's demands and to feed the ball to her instead.

K. D. delivered a perfect pass. Tyra collected it and ran with the ball. She beat two Darnley defenders.

"Go, Tyra!" the boys yelled.

She was ten yards from the goal, inside the penalty box, aware of a third defender coming at her from behind.

Crunch! The Darnley girl went straight for Tyra's legs and brought her down.

Tyra hit the ground and rolled. She jumped up, claiming a foul. The referee nodded. *Penalty!*

This was it—the game-winning moment. All eyes were on Tyra, until Alicia strode up to the penalty spot, ready to shoot.

As the captain, Tyra had a split second to make a decision—should she let Alicia take the kick, or should she step up and take it herself? There was a look in Alicia's eyes that said she would never forgive Tyra if she shamed her by sending her away. *We're a team!* Tyra thought quickly. *This time I give the spotlight to you, Alicia.* She moved aside.

With a triumphant nod, Alicia placed the ball on the spot. She took five paces back and then ran toward the ball.

In the goalmouth, the Darnley goalie crouched, ready.

Alicia kicked the ball low and fast. The goalie dived the right way, her fingertips made contact with the ball, and she flicked it clear.

"Great save!" The Darnley players surrounded their goalkeeper, cheering her.

Tyra felt a sharp jolt of disappointment, but pushed it to one side. "Okay, don't let it get to you," she told Alicia. "Let's keep up the pressure," she said to the rest of the team as the ball came back into play.

The minutes flew by. Soon they were down to ten minutes left, then five, and both teams were tiring. Still zero–zero.

On the sidelines, Mr. Gray had moved up to talk to Mr. Wheeler, no doubt giving him the benefit of his vast experience—pointing, jabbing his finger, and shaking his head.

On the field, Tyra watched Molly's goal kick soar through the air. She received it at the center line and saw that her way ahead was clear except for two Darnley players on the far side of the field. With a swift run, she could reach the goalmouth and take a shot.

Tyra would never know where she found her sudden burst of energy. It was as if her feet had wings as she streaked ahead, smoothly dribbling the ball, focusing on the goal ahead.

The two defenders ran heavily across her path. Tyra easily swerved and outran them. Now there it was—a clear goalmouth. The goalkeeper was off her line, running forward.

Wham! Tyra struck the ball with her right foot. It flew past the goalie into the back of the net.

One–zero! It was a moment of genius. It

won the game.

"Well done!" Mr. Wheeler's smile went from ear to ear as the final whistle blew.

Mr. Gray slouched off, grumbling about a lucky break. Mikey and Adam conceded that Tyra's goal had been pretty cool.

Tyra shook hands with Darnley's captain. She rolled down her socks and walked off the field. There was no feeling to beat this—the moment when you knew you'd played your best and won, and now you could relax and enjoy it.

Molly came up to her and linked arms. "That was a stonker of a goal, cap'n!"

"A 'stonker'?" Tyra laughed.

The rest of the team surrounded her, all except Alicia, who shook her hair out of her ponytail and walked alone toward the changing room.

Then Tyra made out a figure at the back of the crowd. It was her dad in uniform, on his way home from work.

He walked toward her—upright, serious,

but with a faint smile.

Tyra moved away from the team. "Did you see the goal?" she gasped.

Her dad nodded. "You bet."

As always, Tyra had to squeeze out every drop of praise. "What did you think?"

"I think you should have dummied and then shot with your left foot," he told her. "That would have been the icing on the cake."

Tyra grinned at him. "We won the game, Dad! We're on the road to success!"

He nodded and relented. He even put his arm around his daughter's shoulder. "Good job, Tyra. Hey, it's like the sun suddenly came out, and I've got my Florida girl back!"

Chapter 7

"Lucky, lucky, lucky!" Mr. Gray was not happy. He'd just had to stand through Monday morning assembly and listen to the principal praise the girls' team.

"Luck had nothing to do with it," Mr. Wheeler pointed out. He smiled at Tyra as they passed her in the corridor. "Friday's win against Darnley was down to our superior skills!"

"Tell me that in a month's time," Mr. Gray grunted. "After your precious girls have lost a few games and you're lurking at the bottom of the league table again."

No way! Tyra stood in line outside of her French classroom, silently vowing that this was not going to happen.

Molly stood next to her, buzzing with the thrill of the principal's message. He'd singled out her and Tyra for special commendation. Everyone in the assembly room had applauded them. "Let's ask Mr. Wheeler if we can enter the Yorkshire Schools Cup," she suggested.

The line shuffled forward, and they entered the classroom. "What's that?" Tyra asked.

"It's a knockout competition. It takes place during one weekend in October. Our team wasn't good enough to enter last year, but now I reckon we're in with a chance!"

"Sounds cool," Tyra agreed. "Why don't you ask him at practice tonight?"

"No, *you* ask him," Molly insisted. She chose a desk for herself and the one next to it for Tyra. "He's more likely to say yes to you. Since Friday you're his number-one girl!"

"Okay, I'll ask," she agreed as the teacher walked in.

★ ★ ★

"Sir, if we reach the final, we get to play on Manchester United's grounds!" K. D., Diana, and Kim were the first to back up Tyra's request.

"Sir, let's enter. The boys did it last year. They got through to the semis!"

Mr. Wheeler listened carefully. "I'm not sure. Maybe we ought to concentrate on the league," he suggested.

This time Molly jumped in. "Let's do both—the league *and* the cup! We'll work really hard, sir, we promise!"

"Let's see." Their coach checked his diary. "The Yorkshire Schools Cup takes place on October twelfth and thirteenth. As it happens, we don't have a league game that weekend."

"Cool!" Sara and Michelle acted as if the decision was already made. "If we win, do we all get to lift the cup?"

Mr. Wheeler grinned and gave in to the pressure. "Alicia, Emma, Natalie—are you happy with this?"

Reluctantly, they nodded, though Alicia looked as if she'd just sucked on a lemon.

"Good. I'll fill in an entry form and send it later today. Keep your fingers crossed that it's not too late!"

Tyra went in to the second week of training with high hopes. She no longer noticed the lack of skills in some of her teammates and instead saw a whole heap of raw talent. Besides, the entire team, except for Alicia and her two sidekicks, were pulling together, working harder on their running and pushups, getting the hang of the tactics that Mr. Wheeler had taught them.

On Wednesday night they reserved the Astroturf field, and Mr. Wheeler refused to move when Mr. Gray tried to bully them off.

"You didn't sign up on the board," the young teacher reminded him. "You'll see my name there in black and white if you care to look."

So it was the boys' turn to slide around in the mud while their coach fumed and fussed.

Tyra, meanwhile, demonstrated a stretching and flexing exercise that she'd learned with the Butterflies.

"That's useful," Mr. Wheeler said. "Everyone have a try at that."

"Yes, oh wise one!" Alicia scoffed, giving Tyra a mocking curtsy, which Mr. Wheeler caught out of the corner of his eye.

"Not acceptable, Alicia!" He pulled her to one side. "Listen, what's your problem? You need to tell me so I can help sort it out."

"*I* don't have a problem!" she countered, holding his gaze without blinking. "I'd say the problem, if there is one, lies with someone else!"

"Meaning Tyra?"

Alicia continued with the blank stare.

Mr. Wheeler frowned. "That's not the way I see it, Alicia," he said steadily. "I think the issue here is yours, and it comes under the label of envy."

Alicia let out a short hiss of air. "You must be joking!"

"No, I'm dead serious. And in a way, I sympathize. It's always hard when a new, gifted player joins a team . . ."

"Gifted!" Alicia echoed.

Mr. Wheeler's eyes narrowed. "Okay, enough," he decided. "But if this continues, Alicia, I'll be forced to think again about team selection."

"Are you threatening to throw me off the team . . . sir?" The last sarcastic word fell off the end of Alicia's question.

The coach nodded. "That's exactly what I'm doing. So if you value your place, start working *with* your team captain instead of against her, do you hear?"

Okay, so now I have to feel sorry for Alicia, Tyra e-mailed Lacey on Thursday. *Today during lunch break I get this whole sob story from Molly (who, by the way, is cool).*

Figure it out—there has to be some reason behind Alicia and the way she acts, and sure enough, Molly gave it to me straight.

Alicia's mom left home this summer. Yeah, really. She ran off. And pretty soon after this, her dad moved a new girlfriend into the house. This girlfriend is now the queen bee, and believe me, this really annoys Alicia!

Before Alicia's world fell apart—i.e. last year, which was her first year in junior high school—she acted totally different. According to Molly, back then Alicia was the most popular girl in their class. She was so-o-o cool—ahead in the fashion department, good at sports, a teacher's pet. But not now. I hear she's already behind with her work and is in trouble with the teachers.

And guess what? Mr. Wheeler threatened to throw her off the soccer team! I'm serious. Alicia told Natalie, who passed it on to Molly, who told me!

And you know what? I don't want that to happen. I mean, if Mr. Wheeler throws Alicia off the team, the girl has nothing!

Is there something I should do? Write me and give me your views. Love, Tyra xxx

★ ★ ★

Hey, Tyra,

You want my advice? Don't go near the kid. Sure, it sounds harsh, but believe me, she's T-R-O-U-B-L-E!

So, she's not happy. But why turn on you? What did you ever do to her?

This is Little Miss Spoiled Brat we're talking about here.

And listen, a kid like this could do something stupid, big-time. She could wreck things for you, Tyra—I mean it.

So watch out and don't feel sorry for her.

I'm saying this 'cause I know you can be a little naive. Time to toughen up, Tyra.

Love ya!—Lace xxx

"Okay, we're in!" Mr. Wheeler announced before the team's second league game.

It was an away game, and the girls were on the bus to Ryegate, all except for Alicia, who had a dentist's appointment and was due to join them later. It was raining hard, the windows were steamed up, and tension was high. "We've been accepted to play in the Schools Cup."

"Awesome!" Molly jumped up from her seat at the back of the bus. "Just you wait, sir, we'll show the boys that we can do better than them!"

"Yeah, they only got to the semis," Michelle added. "We're going to win this cup if it kills us!"

"Sit down back there!" the driver grumbled as he signaled to turn into the Ryegate school grounds. The wipers of the bus swished, and the tires splashed through deep puddles.

Chatting excitedly about their chances in the Cup, the girls stepped out and began to trail across the wet playground while Mr. Wheeler asked the driver to open up the luggage compartment. Tyra stayed behind to help carry the uniforms.

"Huh!" Mr. Wheeler said, leaning into the hold. "Where did you put the bags, Tyra?"

"In there, sir, like you asked me to." She was certain that there were three sports bags safely stowed—one with neatly ironed shirts, one with shorts, and the third with socks and shin pads. She'd put them there herself. But when she ducked down to take a look, they were nowhere to be seen. "Huh!" she echoed. *What do we do now?*

"Are you sure you put them in the right place?" Mr. Wheeler was scratching his head as he went off to check with the driver.

Completely sure! Tyra remembered carrying the bags one at a time from the side door of the gym to the waiting bus. She'd shoved them way back into the big, dark hold.

Mr. Wheeler came back, shaking his head. "It's a mystery. And there's no time to drive back to school to see if you left them somewhere else by mistake."

"I didn't, sir!" Tyra realized her protest wasn't getting them anywhere. Instead they had to solve what was rapidly turning into a crisis. "Maybe we could borrow some spare uniforms from the Ryegate girls?"

Mr. Wheeler clicked his tongue. "Pity," he muttered. "We don't really want to show up looking like charity cases!"

It was right then that a car pulled into the lot, and Alicia stepped out, fresh from the dentist. "Thanks, Dad," she called, slamming the door and running around to open the trunk. "Guess what I found standing in the rain back at Fernbridge?" she yelled to Mr. Wheeler and Tyra.

"It wouldn't be our uniforms, by any chance?" Mr. Wheeler said, relieved. He rushed to help Alicia lift the three bags out of the trunk.

Tyra saw Alicia give him a special, saucy grin. "Good thing I arranged for Dad to pick me up at the playground," she told him. "I spotted the bags as the bus was leaving, but I was too late to stop you. Anyhow, we just threw them in the trunk and followed!"

"It's a good thing you did," Mr. Wheeler told her, hurrying with the bags into the school.

Tyra frowned and shook her head. This didn't make any sense. Oh, but wait a second, maybe it did! *I've been set up!* she thought.

Quickly, she ran through her rival's version of events. Say Alicia had arrived back at school just in time to see Tyra stashing the bags in the hold. Say she'd suddenly seen a way to make Tyra look bad by sneaking the bags out again when no one was looking. Then she could claim, as she did now, that she'd dropped by later and found the bags sitting there in the rain. So she'd end up the heroine who had saved the day.

But that's so childish! Tyra told herself. Then again, this was Alicia she was talking about. And hadn't Lacey warned her to watch out for Alicia's dirty tricks? Upset, she ran to join Mr. Wheeler and carry one of the bags.

Now, here was something else weird—the bag was bone-dry! If Alicia's story was true, it should have been soaked through from sitting in a puddle in the wet playground. "Mr. Wheeler!" Tyra began.

But Alicia hastily cut her off. "Hurry up, Tyra, and stop trying to make excuses. You messed up, okay!"

"But . . . !" Tyra stopped, fuming inwardly at the nasty trick.

"Alicia's right," Mr. Wheeler agreed. "There's no point holding a conference about what went wrong. The important thing is to get these bags into the changing room and get out onto that field, ready to play a decent game of soccer."

Chapter 8

The Fernbridge team played well and won the game against Ryegate. Their three–zero victory was recorded the following day in a small corner of the local paper's sports page.

"The third goal, scored in the dying moments of the game after a spectacular solo run by Alicia Webb, was the best in the match," the reporter recorded. "Goalkeeper Molly Thomas and attacker Tyra Fraser also put in worthy performances."

"Hey, Tyra, did you see that—we were 'worthy'!" Molly said on the phone.

"Yeah, that kinda stinks!" Tyra laughed, glad that Molly was starting to treat her like a real friend. "But the reporter says there's been a great improvement in the team's performance since last year, so I guess that's good."

"You bet!" Molly agreed. "But I ask you—'worthy'!"

"I know. Listen, Molly, I have to go now." Seeing that her mom was hovering in the narrow hallway, having strapped Shirelle into the back of the car, Tyra put down the phone.

Her mom looked nervous, twisting the wedding rings on her ring finger, obviously wanting to speak to Tyra about something.

"Hey, you're all dressed up!" Tyra checked out her classy black pants and white silk shirt. "Are you going somewhere nice?"

Serena shook her head. "I wish! No, sweetie, I have to drive Shirry into Ryegate to visit a new school there."

Out in the car, Shirelle fiddled with the belt buckle and began to shout.

"What school?" Tyra asked quietly.

"A special-needs school," her mom explained. "I've been meaning to tell you—when we met with Shirry's principal on Monday, she told us that they couldn't handle her behavior here in the local school. You see, they don't have specialist teachers . . ."

"So she has to move . . . again?" The news shocked Tyra. Okay, so Shirry was hard to handle, but these people didn't even seem to have tried. "Mom, that's not right!"

"Honey, I'm only doing what I'm told. They say the school in Ryegate has better facilities . . ."

"Let me out!" Shirelle cried from the back of the car. "Mommy, let me out!"

"Can't they see that all these changes are making her worse?" Tyra demanded. "Why don't they give her more time?"

Serena shook her head helplessly. "Honey, I don't make the education policies here in the U.K."

"Mommy, Mommy!" Shirelle wailed.

"I have to go," her mom said, quickly turning and running to the car. "Your dad will be home from work in half an hour. Be a honey and put some coffee on for him!"

More problems with Shirelle, Tyra wrote to Lacey. *More rain, more cold, more everything bad. Except the soccer.*

Hey, Tyra, what's with the "poor me" attitude? Lacey wrote back. *You gotta cowboy up, girl! Any news on the Alicia front? Hurricane A. left millions of dollars worth of damage here. Dad's busy with the house repairs. Mom's calling realtors in Colorado!*

After the Saturday visit to the special school, Tyra's mom went quiet on the subject. To everyone's relief, Shirelle's mood settled. She watched TV a lot and quietly drew pictures of her favorite cartoon characters.

"See!" Tyra's point was proved. "If you don't poke her and push her around, she can be a sweet kid!"

At school, the principal praised the girls'

soccer team again, and Mr. Gray looked grumpier than ever.

"We only tied one–one against Highfields," Adam told Tyra and Molly. "Mikey got red-carded!"

"Whoa!" Molly laughed out loud. "What did he do?"

"Argued with the ref," Adam reported. "So who do you play this Friday?"

"We play the Highfields girls, at home." Tyra confessed that she had the entire list of games right up to Christmas memorized.

"Hey, you're pretty serious about this captain stuff!" Adam was impressed.

"She's cool!" Molly grinned proudly. "The sky's the limit with our team now that we have Tyra as our captain!"

Fernbridge 4–Highfields 1. The local paper reported the girls' games with increasing interest. They even sent a photographer to the game and then ran a picture of Tyra scoring her second goal. It captured her taking a graceful leap to head the ball into the net.

"Tyra Fraser, a new arrival at the school, looks more and more impressive as the season goes on," the reporter wrote. "A natural athlete, with impressive ball skills and tactical awareness, she leads her team from strength to strength."

"That second goal was a fluke." The following Monday, Alicia was grumbling in a corner of a classroom with Mikey and Emma. Mikey had been dropped from the boys' team and was now focusing all his energy on sucking up to Alicia. "I was the one who beat two defenders and made the pass," Alicia pointed out. "Plus, I scored our fourth goal single-handedly!"

"I saw you," Mikey said. "You were cool!"

"People will soon get peeved with Tyra stealing all the glory," Emma chimed in. "Don't worry, Ally."

"I told you not to call me Ally!" Alicia snapped, walking off with Mikey.

Ouch! Emma felt the blow. It really hurt. She went off in search of Molly. "Alicia's planning something really nasty against Tyra," she snitched.

Molly gasped. "How do you know? When? What?"

"Slow down!" Immediately, Emma regretted acting hastily while she was still smarting from Alicia's snappiness and tried to back off. "I don't know. I made it up. Forget I said anything!"

"No way!" Molly wouldn't let it drop. "Emma, tell me. I mean it—you have to tell me everything you know!"

"It's going to happen before the Schools Cup, which is not this weekend, but the weekend after," Molly told Tyra.

The two girls had met up in the park after school on Thursday. For once, the sun was shining, and the fall trees shone gold and orange.

"Push me faster!" Shirelle demanded

from the spinning merry-go-round.

"I squeezed everything I could out of Emma," Molly went on. "It's got something to do with the game against Beckwith. Something bad, but Alicia didn't even tell Emma exactly what she's got planned."

"I can't believe Alicia really meant it," Tyra murmured, though deep down she was worried. "We're playing for the same team, remember!"

"Faster!" Shirelle cried.

Molly pushed harder. "Yeah, you're right," she muttered. Then she stood up straight and looked Tyra in the eye. "But watch out, okay? Just in case Alicia is crazy enough to try something stupid!"

Beckwith was the best team that Fernbridge had come across so far. They had a player from the Yorkshire Schools team playing for them, and they looked cool in their bright red uniforms, with their sponsors' names emblazoned in white across their backs.

They looked confident, playing on their home field, with a big band of supporters on the sidelines to cheer them on.

"Beck-with! Beck-with!" The chant went up as the teams ran out.

"Okay, remember we have to mark tightly and keep our shape," Mr. Wheeler had reminded the Fernbridge girls in his last-minute team talk. "No solo runs for glory, Alicia. And Tyra, watch the defender who's marking you. She's the tall girl with short fair hair, their number four."

"Tammi Ross," Molly had said, nodding. "She's the one who plays for Yorkshire."

At that moment Tyra had caught a strange, poisonous look on Alicia's face, but she dismissed it. She'd concentrated instead on listening to Mr. Wheeler's instructions and on leading the team out to begin the game.

The whistle blew, and Beckwith took possession. Quickly, they moved the ball up the field, deep into Fernbridge's half.

Molly crouched, ready in goal.

"Go, Beckwith!" the fans yelled.

Kim tackled a Beckwith attacker and failed to stop her. With a swift kick, the ball soared into the goalmouth. There was a melee of red and green shirts. A red attacker got the ball and took a shot at goal.

Molly dived and caught the ball. She drew it in close to her chest and kept it safe.

From the halfway line, Tyra breathed a sigh of relief. She waited for Molly's goal kick, received it, and sprinted right down the center of the field. A defender came in from the left, tall and strong. The tackle came—too high and going for the player, not the ball. Tyra overbalanced and went down. The ref didn't award the free kick; the Beckwith fans cheered. On the sidelines, Mr. Wheeler appealed by waving and pointing. But no flags were up. Play continued.

Back up the field into the Fernbridge goalmouth—another high cross, and the same Beckwith forward as before powered through the defense. This time her shot was deflected and went for a corner. More danger. Tyra ran up to organize the Fernbridge defense. Molly stood alert in goal.

The Beckwith forward took the corner—low and unexpected. It was gathered by a Beckwith forward, who pushed it high and tight into the goalmouth. Two Fernbridge defenders and a Beckwith striker leaped up. The Beckwith player found the ball and headed it past Molly into the net.

Tyra's heart missed a beat. Five minutes into the game, and Fernbridge was already one goal down. *Okay, so we fight back!* she told herself. *We need to dig deep and come up with something really special to win this game!*

At halftime the score line remained the same. Beckwith 1–Fernbridge 0.

Tyra's left thigh bore a large bruise from one of Tammi Ross's heavy tackles. She felt frustrated and tired.

"Good work. You're doing well," Mr. Wheeler assured his team. "They've thrown everything they have at us, and they've only succeeded in breaking our defense once."

Gathering their breath, the Fernbridge players took comfort from the team talk.

"I want you to remember our set pieces. Alicia, play back from your normal position. Feed low passes to Tyra up front. Got that?"

Alicia frowned and nodded.

"Tyra, make the most of any solo opportunity. You have the speed to outrun those defenders. Now, what do we want?"

"We want to win!" the team chanted.

"When do we want it?"

"Now!"

Gradually, the will to win burst through again. Tyra and her team took to the field for the second half with fresh strength.

As Molly walked toward her goalmouth,

she passed Alicia, well out of position and having a muttered conversation with Tammi Ross. "Come on—let's go, Alicia!" she urged.

Quickly, Alicia broke away. The whistle blew, and the second half began.

"Beck-with! Beck-with!" the fans chanted.

But Fernbridge took possession and kept it. They passed tight and short, gradually working their way up the field. Tyra received the ball from K. D. and passed it on to Sara. Sara beat a defender and passed back to Tyra, who spotted a space and ran into it. She took a shot, but the Beckwith keeper blocked it, and the fans cheered. The goalie sent the ball wide onto the right wing, where Tammi Ross took it and ran.

So the game seesawed from one end to the other in a hard-fought stalemate. But Tyra ran tirelessly, fighting for each ball, breaking free and swerving around the defenders, keeping up the pressure on the Beckwith goal. *We can win this!* she told herself. *We keep pressing forward; we go for the goal!*

And at last, 15 minutes from the end of the game, there she was—with the ball, free of obstacles, and a clear goalmouth ahead!

Tyra grabbed her chance. She ran five, ten, 15 yards with the ball, into the penalty area. It was time to shoot.

Then, out of nowhere, recklessly using her height and weight, Tammi Ross tackled. Tyra felt Tammi's right shoe crunch against her left ankle. It twisted violently, and there was a stabbing pain as she went down.

The whistle blew. Fernbridge cried out for a penalty. But Tyra hardly heard. She lay on the ground, curled in a ball, holding her ankle.

"Penalty!" Natalie, Kim, and Alicia surrounded the ref.

Mr. Wheeler came running. He bent

over Tyra. "Okay, let's get you out of here," he decided instantly.

Tyra groaned out a protest, but the coach overruled her. Before she knew it, she was on a stretcher and being carried off the field.

Alicia took the captain's armband from Tyra. And it was Alicia who took the penalty and scored. She saved Fernbridge from their first defeat of the season.

"That's a pretty bad sprain," the doctor at the emergency room at Ryegate General Hospital told Tyra. He held up the x-ray of her ankle to the light. "But luckily there are no broken bones."

Tyra winced as the nurse wrapped the ankle. "How long will this take to heal?" she asked urgently.

"How long is a piece of string?" came the nonchalant answer.

"But will I be okay to play soccer in the Schools Cup next Saturday?" Tyra pitched the all-important question.

The nurse shrugged. "I can't say for sure," she replied. "All I know is that your ankle has swollen up to the size of a tennis ball, and you'll be in an awful lot of pain if you try to do too much with it too soon."

Chapter 9

Back home from the hospital, Tyra retreated to her room. She sat on the bed, her injured leg stretched out, supported by a pillow.

"Don't speak to me," she begged her mom. "This is just so unfair!"

"Molly called," her mom told her. "She asked if you wanted her to visit."

Tyra shook her head. "Tell her thanks, but no."

Her mom hesitated by the door. "Honey, maybe . . . I mean, Molly seems like a really good kid."

"No." She was down. The one thing that had lifted her out of her despair since she arrived in Fernbridge was soccer. And now she couldn't play. "I don't want to see anyone, thanks."

"Not even me?" Shirelle asked, darting into the room. She was wearing her glittery fairy wings. "I can do magic. I can make your leg better!"

For some weird reason, this made Tyra burst into tears.

"Witchy-witchy-woo!" Shirelle cried, waving her imaginary wand.

When their dad came home from the army base, he found Shirry and Tyra sitting on the sofa watching TV together. "Mom called me and told me about your ankle," he told Tyra. "So I figured I'd arrange for you to see the physiotherapist at the base."

Wow, maybe Fairy Shirelle had done the trick! This really was magic—her dad acting this way—like she, Tyra, was this important, in the middle of everything else that was going on with Shirry. "When?" she gasped.

"Starting tomorrow, Saturday, and through into next week for as long as it takes to put this right."

Eagerly, Tyra nodded. "Thanks, Dad!"

"Listen, this guy is the best," he assured her. "He knows every trick in the book to get this ankle good again!"

"Okay, so the trauma to the ankle will begin to reduce over the next twenty-four hours," Joey, the physiotherapist, explained. He'd completed some gentle exercises with Tyra and applied an anti-inflammatory spray. "Soon the swelling will go down." He started to wrap up her ankle tightly.

Tyra grimaced as she risked a glance at the misshapen joint. "I need to be ready for Friday," she insisted.

"Is this a life-or-death situation we have here?" Joey quipped. He was younger than Tyra's dad, relaxed and smiley.

"Worse! I'm the captain of the school soccer team," she explained with a grin.

"Then keep the leg raised, captain. Stay off school on Monday and rest it for forty-eight hours. I'll see you on Monday."

"Yes, sir!" Accepting the wheelchair on offer, Tyra let Joey whiz her out of the treatment room and down the corridor, with her dad in tow.

"By the way, what happened to the player who did this to you?" Joey asked as she hobbled from the chair to the car. "Did you at least get a free kick out of it?"

"Penalty," Tyra told him. "It happened inside the box. The referee said it was a definite foul."

Joey nodded, waving them off. "No doubt about it," he agreed. "A whole lot of planning lies behind inflicting an injury as bad as that!"

"It was so-o-o blatant!" Molly insisted over the phone.

Tyra had lounged around all of Sunday and stayed off school on Monday, paying another visit to the physiotherapist that afternoon. Now it was Monday evening, and her new best friend was filling her in on the day's events.

"Everyone on the team is saying that it was the worst foul they've ever seen," Molly assured her. "They want you back as soon as possible."

"Really? Tell them thanks."

"Except Alicia, of course," Molly added. "But what would you expect?"

"So what's her version of the events?" As she talked, Tyra went through the stretching and rotating exercises that Joey had taught her. She felt that her ankle already had more movement and was less swollen.

"Alicia reckons it wasn't deliberate. She's kind of sticking up for Tammi, who, by the way, did *not* get sent off because that stupid referee was so-o-o biased! And, anyway, Alicia would stick up for her cousin, wouldn't she, especially since she hates your guts in the first place . . ."

"Whoa, hold it!" Tyra wanted Molly to backtrack. "You said Alicia is related to Tammi?"

"Yeah, she's her cousin. Why, what are you thinking? Hey, Tyra, what are you saying? You don't think . . . Alicia wouldn't . . . Would she?"

On Tuesday morning, Tyra insisted on going back to school. "Look, I can put a little weight on my ankle now!" She demonstrated for her mom. "I won't do anything stupid like running around at practice, honest!"

She won the battle and got driven to school by her dad.

"Take it easy," he told her, actually opening the passenger door for her and helping her out.

"Hey, Dad, I can do this!" Tyra insisted. She waved goodbye and then took her time walking across the playground, right up to Emma, Natalie, and Alicia.

The three girls turned to stare at her still-bandaged ankle.

"Not expecting me to show up, huh?"

Tyra grinned. "It's magic what a good physiotherapist can do!"

"Hey, Tyra!" Natalie muttered before sliding away.

By this time, around half a dozen girls from the soccer team had crowded around.

"Tyra, you're walking great already!" Michelle told her. "How cool is that!"

Diana and Sara whooped and clapped.

Tyra grinned and nodded. It felt good to be welcomed this way.

"Our captain's back!" Kim cried.

"Yeah, but she's not ready to play," Alicia pointed out coolly. She turned to K. D. and Molly. "Tonight you two have to take the uniforms home and stick them through the washing machine," she reminded them, making sure that Tyra realized who was the boss now.

Molly frowned. "That's usually the captain's job."

"Yeah, well, I'm the captain now, and I'm delegating," Alicia snapped. "Oh, and

Sara, did you call the newspaper office to tell them that we're playing in the Cup?"

"Don't you just love being bossed around by Princess Alicia?" Molly muttered, grabbing Tyra's arm and walking with her toward the school. "How's the ankle—seriously?" she asked.

Tyra took a deep breath. "There's still a little pain," she admitted. "But, hey, this is only Tuesday!"

"And what are you going to do about this Tammi thing?" Molly went on in a low whisper. "Are you going to tell Mr. Wheeler?"

"What—that Alicia played a lousy trick by arranging to get me injured, just so she can take over as captain?" Tyra laid out what they'd both been thinking, but she still couldn't quite believe it. "Tell him that she planned it with her cousin, and Tammi said she'd do it, for whatever reason? Like, *why* would Tammi take that risk?"

"Because Tammi has read in the paper how good you are, you idiot!" Slowly, Molly spelled it out. "And Beckwith is the favorite to win the Schools Cup this weekend, so Tammi made a deal with Alicia because it would be good to take you out of the equation. They're both so competitive, you wouldn't believe it!"

Tyra shook her head. "Not good!" She sighed. "But, you know, we have no proof . . ."

"Hey, you two, what's with the gossip?" Mikey barged in.

"Nothing. Back off, Mikey!" Molly said. She drew Tyra farther into a corner. "Seriously, Tyra, I saw Alicia muttering with Tammi at the beginning of the second half last Friday. Don't you think we have to tell Mr. Wheeler?"

But Tyra continued shaking her head. "I can't do that," she insisted. "Not without proof."

"Okay, if you won't, I will!" Molly threatened.

"No!"

"Yes! There's Mr. Wheeler going into

assembly now. You just watch me!"

Forced to run after Molly down the corridor, Tyra winced at the pain. *Jeez, I hope I didn't just undo Joey's good work!* she thought. She grabbed ahold of Molly. "Wait. Don't do it. Let me talk to Alicia instead!"

Molly hesitated. "When?"

"Today. Before practice tonight."

"And you'll definitely do it?"

Tyra nodded. "I'll do it. I'll speak to Alicia, face-to-face," she promised.

"Did you do it?" Molly pestered Tyra at lunchtime.

"Not yet. But I will." Tyra was waiting until she could talk to Alicia without anyone else around. The problem was that Alicia was always surrounded by her sidekicks.

"So?" Molly prompted, halfway through the afternoon.

Tyra shook her head. The longer she waited, the harder it seemed to go up and accuse Alicia of playing such a dirty trick.

"Do it—or else!" Molly insisted.

They were walking up the stairs to the science lab. Alicia was ahead of them, with Natalie and Mikey to either side. Emma was lagging slightly behind. She glanced over her shoulder to see Molly and Tyra, and then she slowed down.

"Hey, Emma," Molly muttered.

"Hey, Molly. Tyra, I'm sorry about the injury." Emma looked as if she had more to say, biting her lip and glancing anxiously ahead to see if Alicia was watching. "I told Alicia not to do it."

"Do what?" Tyra slowed down so that she, Molly, and Emma were way behind everyone else.

Molly jumped right in, pinning Emma against the wall. "Alicia planned this with Tammi, didn't she? And you knew!"

Emma nodded.

"Come on—spit it out. Tell us the details!"

"Molly's right," Emma confessed. "I did hear Alicia on the phone with Tammi. She said that Tammi had to go in hard, no matter what. She said that it was the only way to get you off the team before the Schools Cup."

"Proof!" Molly cried triumphantly. She turned to Tyra. "What a low-down, rotten snake!"

Just then, Alicia glanced back. With a look of alarm, she shot ahead and scooted into the lab, quickly disappearing through the door.

Armed with the truth, Tyra felt strangely calm. As Molly fizzed with outrage, she walked quietly after Alicia. She found her in the lab, talking loudly to Mikey about the homework they had to hand in.

"I only answered half the questions," she said with a laugh. "Who cares about the insides of a yucky frog?"

"Alicia, we need to talk," Tyra interrupted. Her nerves were steady; she was not going to let Alicia wiggle away.

"Says who?"

"Me. I say so. I want to know why you set your cousin on me during Friday's game."

She spoke loud enough for the people nearby to hear. There was a gasp and then a hush in the room.

"Hey!" Mikey cut in. "You're not serious! That's ridiculous!"

But Alicia shook her head. "Shut it, Mikey. Did Emma just tell you?" she asked Tyra.

"Yeah. But Molly and I had it figured out already. So how come?"

"Because!" Alicia retorted, suddenly losing it.

"Because what?"

"Because, Tyra Fraser, you're a flashy know-it-all who barges in and takes control—that's why! Because I can't stand the sight of you, if you'd like to know!"

"Wow, Alicia!" K. D. muttered. There was a shock wave throughout the lab.

"OK, so now you all know!" Alicia threw a spectacular tantrum, waving her arms and raising her voice. "Tyra's off the team because of me, okay? So what are you going to do about it?"

"Tell Mr. Wheeler." Kim pointed out the obvious. Everyone muttered their agreement.

For a few seconds, Tyra let Alicia stew. She saw fear in her eyes, behind the histrionics. And she knew that Alicia had lost face for good. "No, we won't tell Mr. Wheeler," she decided.

Alicia let out a gasp, like a balloon deflating. She stared at Tyra like a rabbit in headlights.

"We won't," Tyra repeated steadily. "We'll all stay quiet and keep going as if nothing happened."

Molly pushed through the crowd that had gathered. "Tyra, would you like to explain why you're protecting this little traitor?"

Alicia hung her head.

"Because she's a great soccer player," Tyra answered. "We need her on the team!"

Chapter 10

Joey, the physiotherapist, was an expert in sports injuries. By Wednesday, he'd gotten Tyra's ankle into good enough shape for light training.

"Good to see you back, Tyra." Mr. Wheeler greeted her with a warm smile.

"Glad to be back," she replied. And wow, did she mean it. Every day people were telling her that they were pleased to see her, saying how much she'd been missed. "Tyra, you make sure you're ready for Saturday," K. D. insisted at the start of the training session.

"You bet!" she told her, jogging gently along the sidelines. Yeah, it was cool to be welcomed back, and now Tyra felt guilty for ever having looked down on her teammates. Actually, they were great—every last one of them!

Mr. Gray and his boys passed the group of girls. "I see you've got your star player back, Mr. Wheeler," he said. He strutted on, adding a couple of muttered words as he went.

"What was that, Mr. Gray?" Mr. Wheeler called loudly.

"I said, good luck!" Mr. Gray repeated. "Believe me, for the sake of Fernbridge, I want to see those girls come back with that trophy!"

By Thursday, Tyra felt that her ankle was strong enough for her to join in on some new set pieces that Mr. Wheeler was teaching them.

"Not too much running, Tyra!" the coach warned.

"I'm good!" she assured him, sprinting to collect a ball from the left wing. She was in great shape—her body healed fast. She was ready to go!

"Okay, you're back on the team for Saturday," Mr. Wheeler told her at the end of the session.

Everyone whooped and clapped. High-fives all around.

"I'm putting you back in as captain," Mr. Wheeler went on. "Alicia, are you okay with that?"

Pale and serious, Alicia nodded. She'd hardly spoken a word since the face-off with Tyra in the science lab.

"Good. So, no practice tomorrow evening," the coach announced. "I want you all to take the night off and chill in front of the TV. Get a good night's sleep, ready for Saturday."

"Yes, sir!" the team chorused.

"He said 'chill'!" Molly said to Tyra as they headed for the changing room. "But, hey, it's only Thursday, and I'm already wound up and ready to go!"

"Me, too," Tyra admitted. Friday would

be hard to get through. Time would drag. Every minute of the day, her mind would be on the competition, dreaming about getting out there and going for the goal!

"Excited?" Tyra's mom asked.

She'd gotten through to Friday afternoon. She'd come home from school and was now carefully checking items of the uniforms for tomorrow, watched by Shirelle and her mom, who was leaning against the door.

"This is such a big deal, Mom," she replied, laying each shirt flat on her bed and folding it neatly. "The press will be there, and it means a lot to the whole school. Just think what it'll be like if we win the Cup!"

Her mom smiled. "You go, girl!" she told Tyra, grabbing Shirry and carrying her off for her bath before she put her to bed.

Tyra had just finished packing up the uniforms when she heard her dad arrive home from work. She picked up sounds of a serious conversation down below. "Why didn't you tell me?" came from her mom. "A big decision, but I had to do it . . ." from her dad. And lots of stuff in between that Tyra couldn't quite hear.

She went and stood at the top of the stairs.

"Let me get this straight," her mom was saying. "On Monday you put in a request to your commanding officer to transfer back to Florida for the sake of Shirelle's education?"

Tyra gasped and held her breath. She grabbed ahold of the banister.

"I didn't tell you because I figured it might not happen," her dad said. "But today the answer came through. They agreed to the transfer if we still want it."

"We're going home?" Serena asked, in a stunned tone of voice. "Back to Tampa?"

There was a long silence. "What choice do we have?" Tyra's dad said at last. "It's for Shirelle. Our kid's future is at stake here!"

Lacey, we're coming home! Tyra wrote. She was dazed. It was like a bomb had dropped in the middle of her new life and had blown her apart. *Can you believe it? My dad has asked for a transfer, and we're going back to Florida. And I'm playing in the Schools Cup tomorrow, and I can't get my head straight. I'm going crazy. Deep breath. Whoa!*

For the first time in her life, Tyra ran out onto a soccer field without wanting to be there.

Dressed in her stylish green uniform with the black-and-white socks, wearing the captain's armband, she felt like there was a wall between herself and the events going on around her.

"How do you feel?" Molly asked her, launching into a warm-up exercise while teams in brightly colored uniforms limbered up all around. Coaches coached, referees talked with their linesmen, and parents gathered to cheer on their kids.

"Huh?" Tyra shook her head to try and

clear out the little demons of doubt and distraction.

"How do you feel?" Molly repeated. "How's the ankle?"

"Oh, good, thanks." Tyra forced herself to warm up. *This time next week I'll be on a plane to Florida*, she thought, still not knowing how she felt.

"Hey, Tyra, who do we play in our first game?" K. D. asked as she took off her sweatshirt.

Tyra frowned. "I don't remember," she confessed.

"It's Starbourne," Alicia chipped in. "That's the team that beat us five–zero in the league last year."

I'll be at the mall with Lacey. I'll be on the beach.

"Let's go!" Mr. Wheeler gathered his team, went through their team chant, and then sent them onto the field.

They took up their positions. The referee blew his whistle to start the game. But to Tyra, the whole thing was a blur.

★ ★ ★

"Final score: Starbourne 2–Fernbridge 3." Mr. Wheeler recorded the result in his notebook. "Too close for comfort," he muttered.

"You're a star, Alicia," Mikey told her as she came off the field. "Without those two goals from you, we'd have gone out in the first round!"

Breathing hard, Tyra jogged into the changing room and took refuge inside a toilet stall. *Get a grip!* she told herself. *Focus on the game, you bonehead!*

"Hey, Tyra, are you okay?" It was Molly's voice outside the stall.

Tyra unlocked the door and came out. "I'm good," she muttered.

"Is it your ankle?" Molly persisted. "Don't tell me it's acting up!"

"No." Tyra didn't want to talk. She washed her hands and then pushed past Molly, out into the corridor.

Molly caught up with her. "So what is it?

How come your head was way off in the clouds when we were two–one down to Starbourne?"

"Nothing. I'm okay." They were due to play their second game, and this time Tyra was determined to concentrate.

But the game against Ralton Junior High was no better, and it was again thanks to Alicia scoring from the penalty spot that Fernbridge pulled through.

"Great shot, Alicia!" The team crowded around to congratulate her as the final whistle blew.

Alicia grinned. She was back in the place she loved—the center of attention. "One more game, and we've made it to the semis," she crowed. "Remember, Natalie, look for me in the goalmouth and send in those high passes. I'll be waiting!"

"How's the ankle holding up?" Mr. Wheeler asked Tyra, taking her to one side.

"Good," she said and nodded. She stood, hands on her hips, staring over the coach's right shoulder up at the steep, mist-covered hillside.

"Do you want me to rest you for this next game and save you for the semis and hopefully the final tomorrow?"

"No, definitely not!" she shot back. "I'll do better, I promise."

This time the opposition was strong in attack but weak in defense. At zero–zero with ten minutes to go, Molly saved a great shot from their striker and then rolled the ball to K. D., who forwarded it to Tyra. Her instinct to find space took over, and she streaked ahead. She made a clear 30-yard run and then struck the ball. It zoomed past the goalie into the top left-hand corner of the net.

One–zero to Fernbridge! Tyra was back on top.

"So you get to play at the big stadium?" Tyra's dad asked that evening.

The atmosphere at home was edgy. Stuff was not being said out in the open. Her parents were talking behind closed doors.

"If we win the semi in the morning, we play the final at United's grounds in the afternoon," Tyra answered. She was cleaning her shoes in the kitchen, trying to keep her head clear.

"I have to work until noon, but I'll aim to make it in the afternoon," her dad promised.

"Hey, no problem." *Some dads would move mountains to be there!* she thought bitterly, but she hid her irritation, placed her clean shoes neatly side by side on a sheet of newspaper, and went upstairs to her room.

Tyra, no—I can't believe it! Lacey wrote. *You're coming home! Wow!!! But listen—Mom has found us a place in Colorado. We have to move before Christmas, so I won't be here when you come back. Boo-hoo! How much does that not work out?*

"This semi is the most important game you've ever played," Mr. Wheeler told his team.

"St. Aidan's Academy is a tough team to beat—their defense in particular is rock-solid."

Sunday had dawned clear and bright, with a touch of early frost. But by now the sun had melted the frozen turf, and it was a perfect day for soccer.

"So what do we want?" the coach urged as St. Aidan's came out.

"We want to win!" Fernbridge chanted, leaning forward, arms around each other's shoulders.

"Go, girls!" Mikey, Adam, and practically the entire boys' team had gotten up early to watch the game.

A photographer took pictures. There was a big crowd of excited parents, sisters, and brothers.

"Go, Tyra!" a high voice called above the rest.

Tyra glanced around as she took up her position. And there was Shirelle, a big white scarf wrapped around her neck, dressed in a white woolen hat and pink padded jacket, jumping up and down on the sidelines. Tyra's mom stood next to her, giving Tyra a smile and a wave.

We're going home! Tyra thought with a jolt. *Leaving this place and these people. Never seeing them again! But Lacey won't even be there! What's the point?*

The referee blew her whistle to start the game.

"Go Fernbridge! Go Tyra!" Shirelle yelled.

Alicia took possession of the ball. She ran into two tall defenders and fell at their feet.

"Foul!" K. D. and Emma cried.

Alicia stayed down while Tyra ran to join her.

"Their number four brought her foot up and booted me in the thigh!" Alicia groaned.

"Can you get up?" Anxiously, Tyra helped Alicia to her feet. She needed Alicia to be able to keep playing if they were to have any chance of winning this game. "Test your weight on it," she urged.

Gingerly, Alicia put down her foot and

then nodded. "It's sore, but I'll make it."

"Cowboy up!" Tyra nodded. The two girls exchanged a grin.

Hey! Tyra thought. *Did I imagine that, or did Alicia and I just have a civil conversation?*

"Foul!" K. D. insisted, but the ref hadn't seen it and signaled to play on.

It was the start of a tough game. Both teams played tightly, marking and passing well. Tackles were tough, the ref firm but fair most of the time.

On the sidelines, the fans screamed and yelled their support.

"Go, Tyra!" Shirelle's high voice chirped above the others.

Just before halftime there was a free kick to Fernbridge just outside the penalty area. The St. Aidan's defenders formed a wall. Tyra prepared to take the kick. Alicia, Natalie, and Diana were in the box. It was a great opportunity for a classic set piece. But Tyra knew that she had to clear the ball over the heads of the tall St. Aidan defenders or else curve it around the side of the wall. Which should she do? She made a quick decision, running forward and quickly curving it low and fast. Alicia was ready. She turned and, with a quick, decisive flick, beat the goalkeeper and scored.

One–zero to Fernbridge. And that was enough. They were through to the final.

"You're coming together as a team—at last!" Mr. Wheeler praised them and boosted their confidence as they stood there that same afternoon on the sidelines in the vast stadium. "Alicia and Tyra, you're reading each other well now. Michelle, make sure you stay deep. Natalie, you must find more space on the right wing."

Here they were at United's state-of-the-art stadium. Sunday afternoon. The final of the Yorkshire Schools Cup against last year's league winner, Goldthorpe!

If I go, I go on a high! Tyra told herself. Florida beckoned, but this was here; this was now. She looked out across the smooth green field at the huge stands where knots of fans gathered. *Do I want to leave?* she asked herself. And, almost to her surprise, the definite answer came back—*No!*

The Fernbridge team had arrived on the school bus shortly after lunch, and the size of the place—the scale of the event—had frazzled their already stretched nerves. Emma and K. D. had such bad jitters that they felt sick.

All of the girls got changed in tense silence, lacing up shoes and pulling socks up over shin pads.

"Somebody pinch me!" Molly had muttered. "I can't believe this is real!"

"It's real," Tyra had insisted, feeling suddenly calm. The big event hadn't unnerved her, like it had the others. She couldn't wait to get out there.

And now here they were, emerging from the tunnel onto the field, listening to their coach, trying to spot friends and family in the crowd.

"Sara, Diana—hold possession of the ball in that midfield area . . ."

Mr. Wheeler was giving last-minute advice when Tyra heard a short gasp from Alicia, who sat down suddenly on the turf and then covered by pretending to fiddle with her shoe.

Tyra squatted beside her. "You okay?" she murmured.

Alicia's face was white. There were shocked tears in her eyes. "I just saw my mother!" she whispered.

The runaway mom, the one who'd dumped her family and made room for the new woman! Tyra recalled what Molly had told her. "That's good," she told Alicia uncertainly.

But Alicia shook her head. "I've been refusing to see her for weeks and weeks. What's she doing here?"

"Watching you play soccer! She must have heard that we reached the final."

"I don't want her here." Clasping her

hands around her knees, Alicia tried to control her tears. "Make her go away!"

"I can't do that." Tyra knew she had to talk Alicia through this. "Listen, your mom showed up because she's proud of you. I don't know too much about what's happening, but it seems like she wouldn't be here if she didn't care."

Alicia took a deep breath. "You think?"

Tyra nodded. "I *know*. And you know it too, Alicia. Listen, now that your mom's here, we're going to go out there and play like we've never played before, you and me. We're going to run rings around their defense and put that ball in the back of the net!"

"Yep." Alicia nodded and slowly got to her feet. She kept glancing into the crowd as Mr. Wheeler finished his talk.

Tyra followed her gaze, looking for Shirelle's bright pink jacket and her mom standing beside her. The crowd seemed a long way off, contained behind a high barrier. Yes, there they were—but as yet there was no sign of Tyra's dad.

Oh, no, wait—here he was now, still in uniform, making his way toward the front. "Let's win this thing!" she muttered, and she and Alicia trotted onto the field together.

Goldthorpe was strong. They'd only conceded two goals in the previous rounds of the competition. Their team was full of talented players. Not for nothing were they known as the "Golden Girls" in their deep yellow shirts with the black vertical bands.

Playing against these girls was tougher than anything she'd had to do since she'd been with the Butterflies, Tyra realized. For a start, they could easily outsmart the Fernbridge defense and find a way through to make a shot on goal. In the first five minutes, Molly had to save two shots that were on target, and there was one high pass that hit the crossbar.

The Goldthorpe fans cheered, while the

Fernbridge supporters fell silent.

"Michelle, mark your attacker!" Tyra called out in her role as captain. She felt confident, as if she'd finally arrived in a place she loved. "Good save, Molly. Come on—let's go!"

Willpower alone wouldn't do it, though. As strongly as Tyra urged her team forward, so the opposition held them back. Battles were fought in midfield—hard tackles went in; limbs were stretched to the limit.

"Gold-thorpe! Gold-thorpe, go, go, go!"

"Come on, Fernbridge!"

"Goldthorpe's impressive," the local sports reporter jotted in her notebook. "Plucky Fernbridge defenders stave off first-half attacks."

Official photographers crouched behind both goals.

"Zero–zero," Mr. Wheeler muttered, gathering his team at halftime. "Okay, girls, take it easy; we can do this if we get our tactics right!"

Over on the far side of the field, the Goldthorpe coach talked earnestly to his team.

As Mr. Wheeler gave instructions, Tyra took deep, steady breaths and exercised her ankle.

"Defend deep," Mr. Wheeler insisted. "We need Tyra and Alicia up front, ready for the break, but the rest of you mark tightly and stay back. The vital thing is not to concede a goal!"

"No pressure there, then!" Molly muttered.

"Mr. Wheeler's right," Tyra broke in. "Besides, you have to remember, in this game it's what goes on inside your head that matters."

The whole team turned to her, hanging on every word.

Captain Tyra spoke on, clenching her fists and leaning forward. "Think winning, not losing. We need to go out there with the right mental attitude—we chase every ball; we never give away possession. And never for a second do we let up on the desire to win!"

"Yeah!" Molly muttered, clenching her fists. Tyra seemed to have grown several inches since she began her speech. "You tell 'em, girl!"

Too quickly the referee was waving them back onto the field, and the crowd set up their chants once more.

"Good luck!" Tyra whispered to Molly and the rest of the defense. "Hey, Alicia, let's go!"

Zero–zero in the final. Forty-five minutes and 11 players stood between Fernbridge and glory!

Tyra picked out faces in the crowd, including the principal standing next to Mr. Gray, plus talent scouts from three professional teams.

No pressure! Tyra thought with a wry grin, catching Molly's eye.

Once more Goldthorpe started strongly. But this time the Fernbridge defense was solid. They took possession and fed passes out to Alicia and Tyra as planned.

"Alicia Webb came within striking distance on three occasions," the reporter noted. "Mega talent—a rising soccer superstar," she wrote beside Tyra's name.

The photographers aimed their lenses on the two attackers and clicked.

But still there was a deadlock. Minutes ticked by. The girls ran themselves into the ground.

Then, out of nowhere, Natalie was onto the ball deep in Fernbridge's half. She dribbled free of a Goldthorpe attacker, looked up, and chose between her two strikers, Alicia and Tyra. She passed to Tyra.

This is it! Tyra thought. She knew that they could do it this time.

"Here!" Alicia called, out on the left wing.

Tyra passed, neat and fast. Alicia collected the ball and made a run of 15 yards before a defender threatened her with a lunging tackle. With split-second timing, Alicia fed the ball back to Tyra, jumped the sprawling defender, and ran free.

From Tyra back to Alicia with a quick flick. Back again from Alicia to Tyra, and all the time the two girls were working their way up the field, outwitting the defense and approaching the goal. Tyra glanced up. There was one defender and the goalkeeper in her way. The defender came in hard.

Pass back to Alicia or take a shot? *Shoot!* Tyra told herself. She swung her right foot and made contact. The ball shot past the defender. The goalie had no chance. The ball hit the back of the net.

Alicia's arms were around Tyra's neck, and then Kim and K. D. and Sara jumped on top of them. Tyra went down with the roar of the crowd in her ears. She escaped from underneath a pile of bodies, rolled, jumped, spotted Shirelle's pink jacket, there behind the barrier, and ran toward her family. *Goal!*

And that was the final score: one–zero to Fernbridge.

"Underdogs Raise the Yorkshire Schools Cup!" the reporter wrote in her notebook, planning her headline for the next day's sports page.

Stunned, Tyra led her team to the podium, where an ESFA bigwig handed her the silver trophy. She turned to face where her family was standing and raised it high above her head.

What a moment! What a dream!

Then Alicia grabbed the lid of the cup and put it on her head like a hat, running off with it in crazy celebration. Tyra handed Molly the trophy, and she passed it down the line. Soon the whole team was running after Alicia, cavorting in front of their fans.

And Alicia was calling to her mother across the barrier as her mom called back, clapping. Alicia was grinning and crying at the same time.

"Good work, Mr. Wheeler!" The principal gave due credit to the young coach who had transformed the team's fortunes. Even Mr. Gray managed to look pleased at the girls' success.

Then the moment passed, and it was time to get changed and go home, though the buzz of victory stayed with each and every Fernbridge player.

"Wow!" Molly sighed, leaving the changing room arm in arm with Alicia and Tyra. "What next for Fernbridge?"

"We'll win the league!" Alicia said excitedly. "We're unbeatable!"

Tyra grinned but said nothing as the girls split up to join their families.

"Whee!" Shirelle cried as she ran to Tyra. "Pick me up. Swing me!"

Tyra swung her sister high up into the air. *It's over*, she thought. *We're going home.*

"How does it feel?" her mom asked as they walked up the concrete steps, high into the stadium.

"Cool," she murmured. The stand was empty and silent now. The green oblong shape of the field glowed.

"Good job, Tyra," her dad said quietly.

"But . . ." Tyra sighed.

"But what?"

"But we have to leave, don't we?"

Her dad and mom stopped short. Shirelle ran on ahead.

"How did you know?" Serena asked.

"I heard you say we were moving back to Florida because of Shirry," Tyra confessed. Her lip trembled as she spoke. She wanted to go home to the Tampa Bay Butterflies, even though Lacey wouldn't be there. She wanted to stay here, because of Molly and the Fernbridge soccer team. Heck, she didn't know *what* she wanted.

Her parents stared hard at her.

"You weren't supposed to hear that," her mom murmured.

"I'm way up high!" Shirelle called to them from the very top step.

"Hey, listen!" Tyra's dad stopped her from going up to join Shirelle. "I saw my commanding officer after work today. That's why I was late."

"And?" Tyra asked.

"And he says the army can find good treatment for Shirry here in the U.K."

It was one too many shocks to Tyra's system. She sat down on the step. "They can help her?"

Her mom and dad nodded.

"We can stay?" Tyra asked.

"We figure we should give it a try at the new school in Ryegate," her mom said.

"For at least a year," her dad added.

As Tyra took in the news, Shirelle hopped slowly down toward them. She came and leaned against Tyra's legs.

Tyra stared down at United's field. She imagined a crowd roaring in her ears. She looked ahead to a year of soccer at Fernbridge Junior High.

"Cool!" she whispered, giving her kid sister the biggest hug. "You know what, Shirry—your big sister just won the cup! Now we're going to be at the top of the under-thirteens' league! We're going to be unbeatable."

Want to read more exciting sports stories?
Here's the first chapter from Donna King's
Game, Set, and Match*!*

"You're a winner, Leo, and you have big dreams."

Carrie Springsteen read her horoscope and sighed.

"You get right where the action is, and don't you just love it when the spotlight is on you!"

No! Carrie thought. *Okay, so I have big dreams of winning in tennis, but that spotlight stuff—no way!*

She sat cross-legged on the grassy slope, reading her magazine. Although she had an August birthday, she didn't see herself as a typical Leo show-off. More of a shy type, really.

"Good shot, Joey!" Hilary called across the net to the dark-haired kid she was coaching on a nearby court.

Carrie glanced up, sighed again, and then closed her magazine. Joey's session was about to end. *Me next,* she thought.

Her dad came down the steps from the clubhouse. "Hey, Carrie, why aren't you warming up? Come on, pick up your racket—the summer vacation may have begun, but we can't have you slouching around."

So she sprang onto her feet, and they headed to the practice court. For ten minutes Carrie hit a ball against the concrete wall.

"Nice work!" her dad told her. "That backhand is really improving. Most grown-ups can't hit the ball that hard. Good job!"

Carrie grinned at him. She felt good—ready to start work with Hilary.

"Hi, Carrie!" The coach greeted her with a wide smile. "How's my star player?"

"Great, thanks." Carrie took up her position across the net from Hilary. She checked her grip and waited for the first ball.

Whack! She hit it in the middle of the strings and returned it fast and low.

"Good shot!" Hilary called.

She nodded and smiled. *Yeah, that felt cool!* Carrie pushed a stray strand of fair hair back from her face and tucked it into her ponytail.

"Again!" Hilary instructed.

Whack! Carrie played the same shot. It zoomed across the net.

"Watch your position. Move your feet!" her dad shouted from the sideline.

Carrie nodded. She crouched and waited. The next ball came toward her, and she hit it hard.

"Nice one!" Hilary said, studying Carrie's backhand.

They'd been playing for almost an hour without a break. Carrie's dad made sure that there was no "slouching around," as he called it.

"Move your feet!" he had yelled over and over. "Come on, Carrie! Run!"

It was hot. She was tired. The palm of her racket hand was sticky with sweat.

"We've got the County Championship coming up this weekend," Martin Springsteen reminded Hilary. "Carrie needs to be at the top of her game."

"She's playing really well," the coach told him. "Her backhand drive is her strongest shot. For a twelve-year-old player, it's the best I've seen."

"Yeah, but she still has to work on the rest of her game." Carrie's dad wanted his golden girl to win. He was determined to make her the best. Ever since Carrie had been able to hold a tennis racket, he'd had his heart set on producing a Grand Slam champion.

Hilary glanced up at the hot sun. "Let's take a break," she suggested.

"No, we haven't had our full hour," Martin argued, checking his watch. "Keep playing, Carrie. You need to practice your serve."

★ ★ ★

The hour of coaching was over at last. Carrie was in the changing room, getting ready to take a shower. She unlaced her tennis shoes and threw them under the bench. Then she unzipped her dress and loosened her long hair. Turning on the shower, she tilted her head back and let the cool spray sprinkle her cheeks.

Good shot! . . . Nice serve! . . . Game, set, and match to Carrie Springsteen! For her whole life she'd been hearing that stuff.

Carrie's a natural tennis player . . . She has buckets of talent . . . That girl will go far!

At five years old Carrie had been spotted by the coach at the fancy club where her mum and dad played tennis. At seven she'd been put into a special program for talented tennis kids.

"Carrie's the one to watch," everyone said. "She's a future Grand Slam champion. She's a star!"

Under the shower Carrie could hear all

those voices inside her head.

Okay, at 12 she could hit the ball harder than most adults. She had the longest legs, terrific speed, and lightning-quick reactions. She *was* good!

But lately she didn't go out on the court with a spring in her step like she had last year and all the years before. Carrie took a sharp breath. Maybe she was tennised out!

Take last night, when her best friend, Liv, had called.

"I'm meeting Alice and Mandi in town tomorrow at ten. We're going shopping. Can you come?" she asked.

"Sorry, I can't," Carrie said.

"Okay, don't tell me. You're playing TENNIS." Liv had said the word in capital letters—like, TENNIS MENACE!

"Yeah." Carrie's voice was flat. She was missing out again.

It was the story of her life. Tennis triumph and social life sadness.

Sorry I can't come to the dance/party/ movies . . . I need an early night . . . I'm playing in a tournament. For Carrie, tennis always had to come first.

Sighing, she turned off the shower and got dressed. *Ouch!* She felt a small pain in her thigh, as if she'd pulled a muscle. Pressing her thumbs into the spot, she massaged the ache.

"Hey, Carrie, are you limping?" Hilary asked as she came out of the changing room and onto the balcony overlooking the courts. The coach had been talking with Martin Springsteen while he waited for his daughter to shower and change.

"It's nothing," Carrie answered.

"Are you sure you don't want Hal to take a look?" Hilary asked.

"No, thanks." Hal was the physiotherapist, but Carrie didn't think the pain was serious.

"Probably just a cramp," her dad guessed, taking her sports bag and heading off down the steps toward the car.

For a few seconds Carrie hung back.

"Is everything okay?" Hilary asked. She knew that Carrie was shy and wouldn't always say what she was thinking.

"Yep." Carrie couldn't think of what else to say. Anyway, her dad was waiting.

"Well, good luck in the under-fourteens this Saturday," Hilary said.

Carrie smiled and nodded.

"The County Championship is a good one to win," her coach reminded her. "It'll get you noticed at a national level—the big time!"

Where the action is—the spotlight! Carrie swallowed hard. "Thanks!"

Hilary gazed at Carrie—at her wide, blue eyes and her sunburned face. "You can do it!" she said quietly.

Carrie gave Hilary a final nod before she followed her dad down the steps. The ache in her leg was still there, she noticed.

"Your mum called—lunch is ready," her dad said as she got into the car.

She took out her phone and read her text messages as they drove home.

Gd luck on Sat Alice had texted.

Bought cool shirt Liv wrote.

Cool Carrie texted Liv back. Then she stared out the window while her dad talked tactics for the weekend's matches.

"Plenty of topspin on your second serve . . . good, solid baseline play . . . don't take risks . . . wait for your opponent to make the mistakes . . ."

Yeah, Dad, whatever! she thought. She rubbed the ache on the side of her thigh. *But do you know what? Okay, you and Mum want me to be a tennis star more than anything else in the world. But the way I feel right this minute, I wouldn't care if I never picked up another tennis racket in my whole life!*